MY (MOSTLY) SECRET BABY

PENELOPE BLOOM

Want a free book exclusive to my subscribers? Sign up to my no-spam VIP club and get FREE copy of Miss Matchmaker instantly. Click Here>>

1

DAMON

New York City was exactly the kind of cold I liked this time of year. Dreary, quiet, and with just the slightest touch of depressing. People were too busy clutching their arms around themselves and ducking their heads against the breeze to bother me. No strangers in line at the coffee shop were shooting pairs of finger guns at me while suggesting I smile.

The thought of walking around the streets of New York with a fucking smile on my face was ridiculous. Very few things in this world made me smile—and one of those was a secret I'd take to my grave.

No. I preferred to get shit done. Speaking of which, I took an annoyed glance at the Rolex on my wrist and stepped out of the car. After a second thought, I leaned back in the car window and told my driver to circle back in thirty minutes. Hopefully, that was all the time it'd take to track down my younger brother, Chris, and drag him to the meeting.

If I knew my brother—unfortunately, I did—he'd be somewhere around where I told him to meet me but not quite there. He'd also probably be doing something stupid instead of sitting and waiting like a normal human being.

I swore, he was one of thirty professional athletes I personally represented for my agency, but he was at least ninety percent of the work I did on a daily basis. My little brother was what you'd get if you took the energy and libido of a poorly behaved middle schooler, the sense of humor of an old man, the temperament of that pissed off goose who bites kids at the pond, and put it all in the body of a professional athlete.

I was supposed to meet him outside the Marriott five minutes ago. Of course, there was no sign of him out front, so I had to resort to wandering the sidewalk to see if he'd been distracted by a vendor selling balloons or maybe a hot dog stand. Once, we'd been doing a photo shoot at a museum and I eventually found him in the kid's room organizing some sort of Hot Wheels race between a bunch of toddlers.

That was Chris. High energy, and high fucking stress for me.

Some of the top athletes from around the world were meeting here to discuss potentially joining team USA for next year's Olympics. Ever since I'd started representing my brother as his agent, I'd known I wanted to leave my mark. I wanted to be like Michael Jordan's agent, David Falk. I wanted to do more than take the money sponsors decided to throw my brother's way for what he did on the field. I wanted to make an empire for him. For us.

That brought us to the Marriott. American football still wasn't included in the Summer Olympics, and I was going to make my first attempt today to change that. Just like the Olympic Games had propelled Michael Jordan to stardom, they'd do that for my brother and more. He'd do what he always did and dominate on the field, *and* he'd be remembered as the one who brought American football to the Olympics.

Of course, that all depended on me actually finding the idiot. Besides, if Chris managed to screw this up, which was entirely likely, I could probably poach an athlete or two from their agent while we were here. But that was beside the point.

I did actually find a man selling balloons to a crowd of little kids and their parents. My brother was nowhere to be seen, which meant he'd probably gone inside chasing his other interest: women.

I was about to head into the hotel when I saw a little girl lose hold of her balloon. She let out a squeal of anguish that drew everyone's attention to the little red ball of rubber the wind was carrying directly toward me.

Admittedly, I didn't really want to catch the balloon. If I was telling the full truth, I was a little tempted to pull a pen from my jacket pocket and pop the thing. After all, it'd be a good lesson for her. Hold on to the shit you care about, and don't trust other people not to destroy the things you love. Ultimately, it didn't matter what I wanted to do about the balloon. I had a reputation to uphold.

I was an asshole, and I never planned to apologize for that. Life got complicated if people started expecting you to care. Not giving a shit was the strongest armor out there, and I was decked head to toe in the lack of shits I gave.

So I watched the balloon sail right past me, not even lifting a hand as it drifted by. It blew over a sewer grate and launched upwards, quickly turning into a sad little red dot that was destined to explode in the stratosphere.

I realized the girl's mom was yelling at me and someone was actually filming the whole ordeal on their cell phone—because sure, an angry lady yelling at a guy on the street was going to be riveting entertainment for her twelve Facebook friends.

"Are you—" the lady stammered. Her mouth worked soundlessly like she'd just turned into a fish out of water. "Un-be-liev-able. Do you enjoy making little girls cry?"

Sometimes.

"Are you even going to say anything?" she demanded.

Not if I don't have to.

"I should—I wish you would—" She shook her head, soundless in her outrage as the little girl on her leg finally started to realize her balloon wasn't coming back. Her small face crumpled up and a big, fat, salty tear fell from her chubby cheeks.

Jesus. I held up my hand to shut the mom up and fished in my wallet for something to shut her up. I stuck out a hundred-dollar bill for the little girl. "Go buy another one. And hold onto it next time, or I'll pop it myself."

The mother looked even more outraged, if that was possible. The little girl immediately cheered up and took the money, though. "Let's go buy a car!" the girl said.

With one last dirty look for me, the mother hurried off with her daughter.

"Wow." A young woman in her early twenties was standing beside me with a duffel bag over her shoulder. At another glance, I realized she was some sort of athlete. I guessed tennis from the lean build, somewhat muscular shoulders, and the giant stitched green tennis ball on her bag. She had sun-bleached hair, tan skin, and looked like she belonged on the grass courts of a country club moaning with each stroke she took.

I'd meant the thought to be dismissive, but it stirred up an irritatingly vivid thought of what it'd feel like to take a handful of her hair and listen to her gasp as she stroked something other than fuzzy yellow balls.

"Impressive, I know," I said dryly. I'd perfected the technique of saying "fuck off" without actually saying it. The secret was all in the tone. You could say "have a nice day" and bring someone to tears if you really practiced. So when I started walking toward the hotel, I was surprised she hadn't taken the hint.

She followed. "If you mean your ability to be disgusting and cruel to a little kid? Yeah. It was super impressive."

"Is that all?"

She took two quick steps, putting herself in front of me and placing her fist on her hip. The way she cocked her ass out to the side like that made me want to laugh.

"Does that pose usually frighten people into taking you seriously? Once they get past the whole Barbie aesthetic, I mean."

She pulled a water bottle from her bag, untwisted the cap, and then flicked it toward me. Cold water splashed from my forehead to my chest, but there was nothing cold about the anger that roared up in me. "What the f—"

"Sorry," she shrugged, smiling in a sugary sweet, completely fake way. "I thought if you were actually Satan, water might boil off you or something."

"Wouldn't it need to be holy water? Or do tennis players carry that around in their bags now?"

"I actually just wanted to splash you. Consider it karma for all the little kids you probably stepped on to get out of bed this morning."

I had to give her credit. She had my attention, and that was an accomplishment in itself. But I also knew better than to give my attention to those who demanded it. I needed to ramp up the asshole factor by a few levels to get her out of my life before she caused me problems.

"I didn't get your name."

"It's Chelsea."

"Wonderful. I'll make sure when you eventually decide to take your pathetic career to the next level and get an agent, nobody will work with you. Have a nice day." I'd already given her more energy and words than I cared to waste on strangers, but she seemed to rile me up more than usual.

"No." She planted her other fist on her hip, blocking my way completely, unless I wanted to mow over her.

"No?"

"Yeah. 'No.' Ever heard that? It's what people say when they don't plan to take your shit. It means you don't get to just talk to me like that and expect me to pretend it's okay."

I had to fight back a smile. To tell the truth, I *did* get tired of all the bowing and scraping. Being a ruthless asshole in a position of power quickly turned people into mindless "yes" people. So, in a way, she was right. The word "no" was foreign, but oddly appealing to my ears. It also made me take another look at her. I also couldn't resist screwing with her a little.

"I hear 'no' all the time. When I'm firing people. When I'm ruining their careers. I'll probably hear it as much as I want if I ask any other agents if they've ever heard of you, too."

She smiled in a way that wasn't friendly and bubbly like her unbleached hair and freckled nose would make you expect. It was a challenge. It was a statement that she wasn't cowed in the slightest by my attitude. If anything, it felt like she looked more and more emboldened every time I tried to piss her off.

Yeah, there was a little bit of the boring Barbie look about her. But the closer I looked, the more I wasn't so sure that was quite right. She had slightly imperfect teeth—like she'd had braces at one point and been too stubborn or lazy to keep up with wearing a retainer. Yes, I still wore mine at night, but that was only because I wasn't the sort of dumbass to waste years of orthopedic suffering. Deal with it.

For some reason, she was just standing there, apparently fine with taking my insults and saying nothing.

She also had a little crooked slant to her nose, almost like she'd taken a tennis ball to the face. Or, judging by the way she was insisting on poking the bear at the moment, maybe a fist was more likely.

Whatever it was, I made an executive decision that I'd enjoy knocking her down a peg in a more personal way, especially if she wanted to just stand there looking smug.

"But I have a feeling I could make you say 'yes.'"

"Excuse me?"

"With a little privacy and a few minutes. I'd practically have you screaming it." I wasn't sure if I was even serious, but I knew one thing: her straight back and confidence did things to me. They made me want to push until I found how much it took to make her bend. And *damn,* I had to admit I was starting to wonder how it'd feel to put my hands on her smooth, sun-bronzed skin and do a little bending.

"Not only are you an asshole, you're delusional."

"Suit yourself. I've got more important things to do than argue with a B level tennis player."

She huffed, then hurried after me when I went inside the hotel. I had the room number of the meeting on my phone somewhere but didn't feel like slowing down to find it. I opted to just charge blindly ahead until little miss Barbie decided to give up.

No, the Barbie thing didn't work anymore. If she was lucky, she was three inches over five feet tall, and I wasn't sure how she saw over the net. She was more like Tinkerbell.

Why were the short ones always the most stubborn?

After taking a flight up a random number of stairs and veering through several hallways, I turned to find her trailing behind me. I spread my palms at her, feeling the first signs of my calm beginning to erode away. "What do you want, anyway?"

"I was guessing you knew where you were going if you were so important that you could ruin my career. And I assumed that place was the same place I was going."

I stared. "You don't even know where the meeting is?"

She swallowed, then shifted on her feet. "I know where it is. But I wanted to keep my eye on you."

"I'm sure you did." I started off in another direction, suddenly wishing I'd just looked at where the damn meeting was. "Would you stop fucking following me, Tinkerbell?"

"*Tinkerbell?* And no. I said I'm going to keep my eye on you, and I plan to do that. If you try to talk shit about me to some big agent, I want to be there to explain that you're just the asshole who steals balloons from kids."

"I didn't steal it. I let it fly away, and the kid learned a valuable lesson."

"Yeah. Next time, she should kick grumpy men in expensive suits right in the balls?"

I couldn't deal with this. I yanked open the first door I saw and went inside, closing it before she could follow.

I shouldn't have been remotely surprised when she threw her shoulder against the other side of the door and came flying in before I could lock it, sending us both to the ground in a heap.

2

CHELSEA

You know those moments in life when time slows down? Those crossroads points where you have a chance to look at your life and wonder how the hell you wound up right here at this particular moment? Where all sounds become a ridiculously deep, slow rumble of hilarity? Like the way he was saying, "*Whaaat the fuuuuck*" and I was giggling like a madwoman while we hurtled through the air.

This was one of those moments, I thought, as I rode the asshole in the suit through the air like a very expensively dressed toboggan. He braced my fall about as much as a rock, and my knee might've slipped between his legs as I came down on top of him. He crunched in on himself, rolling and tossing me to the side. That would teach him to drop the green smoothies and enjoy a little ice cream, next time.

"Hey!" I shouted, giving him a shove as I got to my feet.

He popped up with almost comical quickness. His dark eyebrows were squeezed together like he was already imagining all the ways he wanted to dismantle me piece by piece. For a child kicking, foul mouthed asshole, he was admittedly handsome. Even if I deducted something like ten or twenty points off the attractiveness scale for obvious personality faults, he still clocked in at a ten out of ten, and that made me hate him even more.

He was one of those guys that was obnoxiously blessed by nature. He had the posture of a soldier with a straight back, neck, and the sort of lean muscularity I'd always preferred on men. Basically, if they couldn't wipe their own asses, they needed to take a break from the gym, and I was fairly sure Mr. Grump could reach his ass just fine with those long... *Stop. And please, Chelsea, for the love of God, never picture a hot stranger wiping their own ass again. That's not good for anybody.*

The point was, the more I looked at him, the more I found for my eyes to enjoy. He had a defined nose, a little mole to the side of his mouth that was, of course, oddly appealing. He even had this sort of bow shape to his full lips that was doing dangerous things in my brain. To top it all off, he had nearly black, perfect hair and a pair of blue eyes bright enough to read a book by under the blankets.

"Hey?" For the first time, he didn't sound icy and calm. "You have got to be the most insane, f—"

"Who shuts a door on someone in the middle of a conversation?"

"It wasn't a conversation! I was trying to get away from you."

"Which one is it? You want to get away, or you want to prove to your fragile ego that you can make me say 'yes?'"

His eyes narrowed into little slits, which made the corners of his cheeks crinkle in a frustratingly sexy way. And just like that, all the fuming anger I'd felt—not just toward him but about the whole situation that led to me coming here today—seemed to flicker and shift inside me. My belly went hot, and my knees threatened to turn soft.

Stop it, knees. We've practiced this whole standing thing a couple times, so don't pretend to be incompetent on me now.

"I should leave you alone," I said quietly. I reached for the door, but he pressed his palm to it, stopping me.

"You don't get to talk to me the way you did and walk away, Chelsea."

I swallowed. I was the most stubborn person I knew. He thought he could rock my world. I saw it in his eyes. I'd challenged him, and he thought sleeping with me would put me in my place. Like coaxing a few moans from my lips while he glared dispassionately down at me would prove some kind of point.

If I'd been even a little less stubborn, I'd have walked away. I'd have known sleeping with someone to win an argument was off the charts of stupidity.

But... I wasn't less stubborn. In fact, I was the kind of stubborn that had resulted in more than a few emergency room trips, like the time I put my tongue on the frozen basketball pole to prove it wouldn't stick—*it did*. Or the time I just had to prove the lake wasn't too thin to ice skate on—*it was*. Or even the time I claimed I could handle a raw ghost pepper—*I couldn't*.

So I reached out and gripped his tie, tugging him a little closer. "Think you'll win this, Mr. Suit?"

His lips curled up at the corners. "I know I will. Just like everyone who winds up across from you on the court probably does."

"You don't know the first thing about me."

"I know you're going to let me kiss you."

I clenched my teeth. I wanted to tell him he was wrong, but when he dipped his chin toward me, and I caught a hint of his manly musk—a scent somewhere between money and fresh cut wood, the words died on my lips.

God. Why was I so stubborn? Couldn't I maybe stubbornly decide to prove I wasn't stubborn, for once? Except all my thoughts felt powerless. I was swept up in him, and deep down, I knew there was no breaking free of this. He was the riptide, and the harder you fought the riptide, the more it had you. The only way out was to relax. Surrender to it and ride out the current until it finally tired of you and let you swim back to shore.

I'd lost the moment I walked into this, but I still wasn't ready to accept that.

I tilted my chin up and let his lips crash down on mine. I wondered if he felt the same rush of white-hot excitement I did in that moment. It wasn't an ordinary kiss. It wasn't two people seeking affection. There was no hunger for approval.

It was a battle, and our lips were the soldiers, battering themselves against each other. Our tongues clashed, slashing against each other in a hot, swirling form of combat that made my body zing with energy.

I tugged at his suit, hoping to tear something while he yanked at my skirt.

When it didn't budge downward, he pushed it up in impatience, hiking up one of my legs and pressing me to the door so he could grind himself against me. His lips brushed my neck and I felt him smile his devil's smile. "Tell me to stop. I dare you."

"You're a baby puncher. And I'm not going to give you what you want."

"No?" His hand cupped me between my legs, making me gasp. "You're already soaked for me."

"That was for someone else."

For a second, I thought he was actually going to laugh, but instead he took me by the shoulder and turned me, pressing my cheek to the wall and forcing my ass against his crotch. "Doesn't matter who you think any of this was for. I'm taking it."

A chill spiked across my spine. Okay. Grumpy? Yes. Arrogant? Definitely. Kid kicker? Probably. But his growly possessiveness was a turn on. I had to give him that.

I licked my lips. "I'm only letting you do this to see your face when you can't make me cum." The truth was I'd never had a real orgasm with a man before. Some happy little butterflies here and there and a few things in between, but never a true orgasm. They'd left me wanting and unfulfilled, and it was half the reason I knew I was going to enjoy this. Watching Mr.

Suit struggle to please me was at least going to feel like a victory.

"I'm not just going to make you cum all over my cock. I'm going to make you wait to do it until you have permission."

I laughed, except the sound didn't have quite the authenticity I was going for. His hands were on my hips and my body was pinned by him. I could talk all I wanted, but I knew I was in his control. His power.

I heard the jingle of his belt and felt the shifting of his pants behind me. I closed my eyes, waiting. I had just enough time to take a look in my mental mirror and ask what the hell I thought I was doing. But everything about today was already a shitshow, starting with showing up to this meeting uninvited. It almost seemed fitting that I was about to hate fuck a stranger in a random conference room.

"I hope you have a rubber, or you're not going near me with that."

I realized I still didn't even know his name as he lazily produced a wrapper from his jacket pocket. *Charming.* I knew I was really scraping the bottom of the barrel when the guy I was about to let inside me was carrying around a personal supply of condoms.

Then again, when you looked like Mr. Suit, having a supply of condoms probably made as much sense as carrying an umbrella around in London.

I braced for him to jam himself unceremoniously into me, but instead I felt both his palms on my ass. I turned to see what he was doing just in time to catch him crouching down behind me and yanking my panties down.

My eyes went wide as he pressed his mouth between my legs and started to kiss and lick the ever-living hell out of me. I tried and failed to dig my fingers into the wall for support. I ended up biting down on my knuckles to stop from moaning in a way I knew would plaster a satisfied smirk on his stupid face.

Yeah. It felt amazing. It was kinda like he was taking his anger out... on my pussy... with his tongue. I mean, if this was the way he vented his frustrations, I guess I could imagine some kind of arrangement where I volunteer to be his punching bag. Especially if the punches would always be delivered by his tongue.

Still, I mustered up the power to stay silent. Every moment I didn't make a sound only seemed to enrage him further. He slid a hand around and started drawing glorious little circles around my clit, but I only bit down harder on my knuckles.

I was the silent night. I was one of those royal guards who didn't flinch. I was... Well, I was in heaven, but it was the devil himself dragging me there, and I was pretty sure you were doing something wrong if the devil took you to heaven.

He made a frustrated sound that vibrated straight into me, stood, and fumbled with something. A moment later, I felt the warm silky pressure of his length sliding between my legs. He took my hands—which also meant removing one of my weapons of silence—and pressed them one on top of the other over my head. With one hand, he held them firmly in place. With the other, he gripped my ass.

Now, I wasn't about to go making claims like the way he felt inside me was the best thing I'd ever experienced. I wasn't going to say it was like somebody mixed together the thrill of a rollercoaster, the butterflies of a first kiss, fireworks, and eating fresh baked brownies into a syringe and injected it directly into my veins. No. I definitely wasn't going to say a word of that. I'd just think it in the privacy of my own damn mind, because *wow*.

My whole body shook as he gripped my wrists and my hip, gliding into me and stretching me in a way that made me feel like I should probably spend the next few years bowing my head in church and begging forgiveness. Because if I'd learned anything from my forced stay in Sunday school as a kid, it was if anything felt this good, it was one hundred percent a sin.

I clamped my teeth together, bracing against the determined

thrusts from Mr. Suit behind me. It was *almost* exactly like I'd imagined. Him frustrated and determined while I was stony faced and unaffected by his efforts. Except he was breathing heavy now and there was nothing stony about the lust-filled heaviness of his eyes.

And I realized with sudden horror that an orgasm was rapidly rising inside me and threatening to explode. All over him. All over my idea that the reason I couldn't get off with a guy was just that the right one hadn't come along—that Mr. Perfect's penis would be the secret key to my pleasure.

This was all wrong.

I lost concentration just long enough for the fated words to slip from my lips. "Yes, oh *God*, yes." *Shit*. I couldn't even press a hand to my mouth because he was pinning them. I felt him tense, and from the way his grip went tight, I realized he had finished inside me. Thank God I insisted on a condom.

He pulled himself out, discarded the condom in a nearby trashcan, and yanked his expensive pants back up like he didn't even care that my arousal was still all over him. Or maybe he was the kind of kinky bastard who liked the idea of walking around all day with me on his cock. I swallowed, wishing that idea didn't turn me on.

I tugged my skirt down, doing an undignified little shimmy before kneeling and pulling my panties up. There was no sexy or classy way to try to put myself back together in front of him. Not after that. Especially not after he'd won our stupid, ridiculous little game.

"Aren't you going to gloat?" I asked.

"No." He straightened his tie, and from the look on his face, you would never know he just blew his load inside me. "I got what I came for."

Stupid, cocky bastard. "Yeah?" I said, sounding a little too desperate to get something from him before he walked straight out of my life. "You're just going to leave?"

He moved past me, pulling the door open and stopping just before he left. "Relationships are for people with time."

"Yeah," I called after him. "And functioning hearts." I didn't know why I was trying to argue with him. There was zero percent of me that thought he and I had even the most remote chance of being compatible in a relationship.

Except... That hadn't just been sex. It was an experience. It had felt life changing, as overly dramatic as that was. He'd swept into my life and in a few glorious thrusts, he'd unraveled one of my most central theories of the universe. My spell of orgasmless relationships hadn't been because the right guy was still out there. It was just—*ugh*. I didn't even know what it was, but now I could never change the fact that *he* had been the one to make it happen. I wished that didn't feel significant somehow.

The door shut, and all I could do was sit down on the cold floor and pull my knees up to my chest. I thought I could feel my life threatening to crack at the seams. And then I felt a strange, warm, and wet sensation between my legs. I shifted a little. I definitely wasn't still turned on, so it wasn't like the old girl was still prepping the tunnel for a train.

I put my hand to the source and flinched. Was that... I pulled it back and saw a little fragment of a condom on my fingertip, along with a generous helping of Mr. Suit's DNA. Before the true shock and horror really settled in, I wondered what kind of supermodel kids were swimming around on my fingertip, just waiting to catwalk into the world and start ripping people new assholes.

I flicked my finger and scooted back, shuddering all over.

The condom broke.

"It broke," I said it aloud, just because that's what my shocked brain seemed to think it needed to do. "The fucking condom broke. He came inside me."

I jumped up and put both my hands on my head. I did some frantic calendar counting and determined that I shouldn't be ovulating. And thank God for that, because I read this terrifying article about what Plan B does to your body once. I swore I'd never touch the stuff after that, except this might've justified an exception.

I briefly thought about running after him and telling him the truth—of slapping his shitty quality jacket pocket condom remains in his face. But no. I just needed to calm down. Biology was on my side. It was *okay.* I'd get tested to make sure I was still clean, and that would be that.

Note from my future self: you see where this is going, right?

3

DAMON

I wasn't particularly proud of it, but I was the king of the one and done routine. If I had my way, I'd eradicate the biological urge to stick my dick in warm, wet holes entirely. As it was, I couldn't do that, which meant I occasionally took detours. The more temporary, the better.

Except my little session of bumping uglies with tennis Tinkerbell felt like the kind of detour I could get used to taking. I liked that she had stood up to me. Of course, she'd ultimately folded like all of them did, but the resistance had been a welcome change. It was also entirely possible I'd just enjoyed fucking her and the rest were excuses to pursue a second-round performance.

I straightened my tie and double checked that my belt was in place. Whether I would've liked to revisit Chelsea again at some point in the future, it was irrelevant. I couldn't afford to tie myself down with commitments, and she'd only disappoint me at best and betray me at worst.

The only thing to do was move on and leave her where she belonged: my past.

When I found Chris, his hair was a mess, like usual, and he was trailed by a long-legged woman in a skin-tight dress.

Chris was a quarterback in the NFL, and he'd always had a way with girls, even before he was rich and famous. It was probably the rugged bad boy aesthetic he had going on. Tattooed, muscular, and quick with a joke. He also occasionally needed guidance like an over-eager dog, but as his bigger brother, that was a job I was willing to take.

He caught my eye, tugged the woman in for a quick, playful kiss on the neck, then waved. "Call me in a few hours. I've got to hydrate and pop a zinc pill before tonight."

I almost made the wise decision and didn't ask, but curiosity got the better of me. "Zinc?"

"Yeah. It helps raise your sperm production. Like volume, I mean." He spread the fingers of one hand and made a popping sound, then mimicked something splattering all over his face and chest.

I squinted. "You want to come all over yourself more aggressively?"

Chris snorted. "No. I never let it touch my own body. Do you?"

"What?"

"When you jack off. Do you spray it on your stomach? Because... I don't want to judge or anything, but I mean—"

"Oh get over yourself," I said, shaking my head in disbelief both at my brother and at myself for knowingly walking into such an idiotic conversation.

He patted and squeezed my shoulder. "Zinc. You should try it. Some girls go crazy for a little DNA shower."

I nearly gagged but couldn't stop from chuckling instead. "I'm almost positive if you ever called it that, *no* girls would love a 'DNA shower.'"

"Well, I'm assuming you didn't come track me down to talk about the contents of my balls. So what's up?"

"You're supposed to be at the meeting. With me. Did you even remember why you were here?"

Chris had sandy blond hair and a strong, square jaw with

vertical lines that dimpled in his cheeks when he smirked—which was most of the time. He reached out and pulled one of my lapels a little straighter. Then he licked his finger and tried to flatten part of my hair. "Strange how you were M.I.A. as well. It's not like the Terminator to take this long to find me. Almost like you were scrotum deep in your own business for a little there." Chris leaned in and sniffed the air. "Hmm. It's not strange that you smell like pussy, you know, given how you are. What's strange is you smell like someone else's pussy."

"You're an imbecile. And it took me half an hour to find you because I had to check the balloon vendor outside for you before I could search the hotel."

"Were they folding them into shapes? Because the last balloon guy I saw said he couldn't do a giant penis and I really want one."

I stared.

"Not for *me*," he laughed a little nervously. "I wanted to give it to you. Just the thought of how happy it'd make you, you know."

"Come on, we're already late enough as it is. If I'm going to have any chance of getting you to the Olympics, we need to show our faces."

"You forget I couldn't give a shit about playing in the Olympics."

"As your agent, I advise you to give a shit. Right now you're just a cog in the machine of your team. Getting you out there as the pioneer who brought the NFL to the world—"

Chris was already looking past me to a young woman in a navy-blue skirt. "Yeah," he said quietly. "I remember your little ra-ra speech. Global brand. Legacy. Yada yada."

I had my hand on the door to the conference room when I noticed a small figure half jogging toward us.

Chelsea.

My dick stiffened when I thought about how I'd just been inside her, and to know the way her hair was laying funny was from when I'd taken a generous fistful. It was like a secret mark I'd left on her, and I liked the way that felt far more than was safe.

She let me open the door for her, then gave a challenging little stare as she passed me and headed into the room.

I stopped her with a hand on her arm before she could get away. Touching her seemed to make the pieces click in place—the way she'd followed me even when I was going the wrong way. The strange looks. I thought I understood, so I took a stab in the dark. "You weren't even invited to this. Were you?"

Chelsea hesitated, then decided to lead with the stubborn edge that seemed to be her default. "No. But I just showed up with some hot shot agent and the most famous QB in the NFL. I'm guessing nobody is going to ask too many questions."

"Like hell you did."

She gestured toward the only three open chairs lined up at the end of the long rectangular table. A woman in business attire was standing and presenting some sort of graphic on fan attendance globally, and our entry only drew a few glances. There were about fifty people in the room, most of which were top athletes in their fields and their agents.

I wasn't blind to my brother's curious looks as Chelsea followed us and sat at my side, but I ignored him and the questions he was clearly dying to ask.

"What happens if I out you to the whole room?" I whispered.

"I don't know. Let's find out." She stared back at me, her smooth jaw flexing slightly as she was undoubtedly clenching her teeth.

"Is that all it was? A ticket to this room?" I leaned in closer, whisper yelling. I shouldn't have felt even slightly offended, but the idea that she'd fucked me and used me felt like acid in my chest. It wouldn't have been the first time, and I'd promised myself not to let women use me again. It pissed me off that I hadn't seen through her soon enough.

"What we did?" She stared back at me defiantly, even as a

slight shade of red splotched across her cheeks. "That was me being too stubborn for my own good. *And it was a mistake.* But I—"

"Shh," a man hissed across the table from us.

"Fuck you," I growled.

The exchange stopped the woman presenting and drew her attention toward us. "Mr. Rose. I'm glad you could join us, but if you would be so kind as to behave, we'll be able to get through the presentation sooner."

I spread my palms. "Be my guest. But I'd like someone to remove this woman before we continue."

"And who is this?"

"I'm Chelsea Cross. And I—"

The director waved her hand, cutting Chelsea off. "I don't know how you got here or why, but you can either leave on your own or I can call security."

Chelsea folded her arms. "Security, then."

With a sigh, the director pulled out her phone and shot me an icy look, as if this was *my* fault.

The whole room sat in tense silence while we waited for security.

Chris broke the quiet, leaning forward on the table to look over at Chelsea, who was sitting with a pissed off expression on her face. "The first requirement of being an athlete is having balls. And you've got a couple."

I nudged him. "Don't encourage her."

"It's a pun," Chris was smirking. "You know. She's got tennis balls in that bag, I'm assuming. And maybe you could confirm or deny if she's got some between her legs as well. Since you two—"

I pressed my palm to his mouth. The rest of the gathered athletes and their representation were watching our little train wreck with interest by now.

"Mr. Rose. What is he talking about?"

Chelsea shrugged. "Maybe the quick sex he and I had right

before this meeting. He was certainly eager to pull his dick out for me after we'd known each other a few seconds. There's a small mole at the base of it, if you don't believe me. I bet he'll be happy to produce his pride and joy for you to confirm."

"Unbelievable." I clenched my teeth to stop the string of curses that threatened to burst out of me. "Can I have a moment with you? Outside?"

She stood, gesturing for the door. "Certainly. But if it's anything like the first time, it'll be a quick moment."

"Roasted!" Chris said, slamming his fist on the table and barking a laugh.

I half pushed Chelsea out of the room and jammed my finger toward Chris. "You're not helping."

He held up his palms in innocence. "Neither is the massive hard on you're sporting from being within five feet of her."

Stupidly, I glanced down to confirm I wasn't tenting my pants.

Chris laughed. "He actually looked. This guy—"

I slammed the door, then rounded on Chelsea so her back was against the wall. "Are you trying to piss me off?"

"Kind of irrelevant, isn't it? Do your nostrils always flare when you get mad? It's kind of cute."

I pushed off the wall and walked a circle with my hands on my hips. She had no idea how much money was at stake in there. She had no idea how much thought I'd put into this transition in my brother's career—and by extension, *my* career. "I want you out of my life."

"In that case, there's something I should probably tell you."

I shook my head, pointing to the security that was finally coming down the hall. "No. You probably shouldn't. Why don't you go back to being irrelevant?"

I knew I had to be imagining things, but her eyes looked almost watery. She licked her lips, paused, then nodded. "Suit yourself. I hope you have a horrible life, cockmuncher."

I scrunched my eyebrows together. Where the hell did this

woman come from? I almost wondered if my brother had fed information to her on how to most efficiently get under my skin.

Security took her by the arms and led her away, but not before she could shout one last thing over her shoulder to me. "You're not even that hot. You have chicken wing shoulder blades!"

I let out a long sigh through my nose, but before I stepped back into the conference room, I tried to adjust my posture. Chicken wing shoulder blades? What the fuck did that even mean?

It didn't matter. By tomorrow, I'd forget all about Chelsea Cross and her brief but fiery interruption of my life. That's all she was. Like an asteroid burning up in the atmosphere before it could touch ground. Distracting, bright, oddly fascinating to look at, but ultimately meaningless.

4

CHELSEA

FIVE YEARS LATER

Somebody once told me to make a list of the things I'd give up my life for. Take a look at that list, they said, and you'd have your compass to live by. You'd know exactly what you valued. What was worth giving everything up for.

Call me a bad child if you wanted, but I wouldn't die for my parents without question. Would I risk my life to save them? Sure. Would I take a bullet for them? Sure. Maybe even two bullets if they were a low caliber.

My dad might only get one bullet from me, because I swore when I was fifteen, I'd never forgive him for smashing my phone. Call me a woman of my word.

But there *was* something in my life I'd die for without question. That little something was currently snarling at me from the backseat of my car.

I tipped my rearview while we waited at a red light so I could see her. She had dark hair and the most stunning blue eyes I'd ever seen. She was quick with a smile and just as quick with her temper.

"I'm gonna knock you out, *momma*."

I quirked an eyebrow into the mirror. "I'd like to see that, considering you're strapped into a carseat. Tough guy."

She curled her lip and made a fierce show of struggling against her harness. "For now."

I choked on my water, laughing. "Who even are you?"

She snarled again. "A monster. A big one."

I may have been stuck in traffic. I may have been struggling to keep a roof over our heads. I may have been trying and failing to do the whole single mom thing with grace. But it was the little moments that reminded me why she was worth everything.

That was Luna. She was the only thing on my list. The little package I'd close my eyes and step off the roof for without an ounce of regret.

In a lot of ways, I guess I'd already sacrificed one part of my life for her. Deciding to keep her had been one of the harder decisions of my life, and it had certainly cost me. It cost me my budding tennis career. It cost me relationships, namely with my parents, who thought I shouldn't keep a kid when the dad wasn't in the picture.

It had also cost me a few tough lessons. When she was born, I'd made the mistake of thinking I could still date men like I used to. It only took a few bad experiences to show me that I wasn't just dating for me anymore. I was dating for both of us. I couldn't settle for the bad boy with a disregard for authority anymore. I couldn't enjoy a few months with the hot mess that doesn't have his life together but makes me smile.

I needed responsible. I needed good. I needed stability, and so far, that was about as likely as finding a bra I didn't want to strip off and light up with a machine gun by the end of my day.

I pulled up to my brother's apartment. I parked on the street and bent to get Luna out of her carseat, except she'd apparently figured out how to do that herself. She curled her little fingers, hissed, and swiped at me. I barely dodged in time, laughing. "How did you learn to do that?"

"Uncle Grant taught me." She wiggled her eyebrows like she was the coolest person on the planet. "I'm bodini."

I grinned. "Houdini. And yes, you are."

My brother ambled down the steps of his stoop, tickling my sides from behind. I straightened and made an undignified sound, then turned to swing at him. He easily bobbed and weaved my attempts, then play slapped me on the side of the head before pulling me in for a hug.

Before his life went off the rails, Grant was on track to be a mixed martial artist. But one thing led to another, and now we found ourselves here. He wasn't the buff, athletic older brother I'd grown up knowing. Now he was thin as a rail and gaunt in the cheeks with pink rims around his eyes.

I still trusted him with Luna. Grant was only a danger to himself, and he'd always been fiercely loyal to everyone he loved.

He scooped her up and blew a raspberry in her belly. Luna tried to knee him in the chin, but as was their routine, the two of them broke into a slow-motion fighting sequence, complete with Grant's exaggerated sound effects.

I watched it all, wishing I could stay and enjoy the time. I knew Luna would make him play monster when they got inside, and it was always fun to see them goof around together. "I gotta get going. Everything is in her—"

"Bag. I know, Chels. Get out of here, and I'll cross my fingers that your shitty car doesn't blow up before you make it to your interview."

"Swear jar!" Luna said, clapping excitedly. Every time Grant swore, he gave Luna a nickel. Unfortunately, he'd taken this as an excuse to swear as much as he wanted around her with the excuse that he was helping her out.

"Here." I pulled a twenty dollar bill out of my purse and handed it to Grant.

He frowned at it. "You sure?"

"She's got to eat. You do, too."

He worked his mouth to the side, then nodded, taking the money. I knew it meant I was probably going to be skipping lunch today, but I also knew the state of my brother's pantry and fridge.

I got back in my car, then took the sort of deep breath you took just before jumping into a freezing pool. I'd taken all the kinds of jobs I could imagine taking to avoid going *there*, but I'd reached a point of absolute desperation. I'd coached tennis lessons, waited tables, mixed drinks, and even picked up dog poop. But I was getting less hours across the board, and it was time to try to land the kind of job that wouldn't require my closet to be packed with more uniforms than personal clothes.

I STEPPED INSIDE ROSE ATHLETIC REPRESENTATIVES, OR *RAR*, AS I lamely enjoyed calling it. The building practically screamed *you do not belong*, from the smells to the way the receptionist was dressed.

I cleared my throat and straightened the skirt I'd been thrilled to find on clearance. It fell to just above my knees but was made of a comfortable stretchy material that looked good without feeling constrictive. I was sure everyone here could still tell I was poor, but I didn't need to focus on that.

It was all completely fine. Nothing to panic about. No reason to mentally run through the procedure for walking like a normal human being again. *Straight spine. Pull my head back for good posture, but not so good that I was rocking a double chin. Act like my arms aren't glued to my sides.*

When I was feeling insecure, I always thought back to the way Elsa from *Frozen* walked once she let her hair down. *The lady walk*, as I called it. And so, I imagined releasing my not-so-luxurious locks and walked toward the reception desk like I'd just magicked the shit out of the place. *Damon Rose never bothered me anyway*, or something like that.

No. He just defied the laws of probability and put a baby in me, broken condom and no ovulation be damned.

The woman—a twenty something like me with brown hair—gave me an expectant look. "Do you have an appointment?"

"An interview, actually."

"With whom?" I hated how her tone said everything she was too professional to say aloud. *You're not getting a job here looking like that. Are you really dumb enough to think you would?*

"Jason. From HR."

She tapped her keyboard for a few seconds, giving me a moment to take in her perfectly manicured fingernails. Well, on the bright side, even the secretaries here were making enough money to keep up appearances. Maybe I could take this girl's beauty budget and pay for a chunk of daycare. *Probably not.*

"Jason is out today. Do you want to reschedule?"

I put my hands on the desk to brace myself. Did Jason realize how much I was putting my brother out to ask him to watch Luna on short notice? "Could I possibly interview with someone else?"

I heard the doors open behind me and felt a subtle change come over the room. The receptionist slid her eyes past my face and focused on something in the distance. She went visibly straighter as she adjusted her hair and puckered her lips a little.

I followed her eyes.

I'd been prepared for this from the moment I decided to apply here, so it shouldn't have come as a shock to see him. But my stomach still sank into a pit of fiery anger when I saw Damon Rose himself storming through the lobby. It had been almost five years now since our little encounter, and he was one of those obnoxious men that only became more distinguished with age. He'd been in his late twenties then, and now he had a hint of lines where there had been none before as well as a little more muscle on his lean frame. I still reckoned he could wipe his own ass, for the record.

Damon was on his phone, and from the sounds of his deep, gravelly voice, he was in the middle of chewing someone out.

The receptionist seemed to remember to do her job after a few seconds. She smiled slightly, then pursed her lips as she shook her head. "I'm sorry. The interview will have to wait until Jason can reschedule, but if—"

"What's going on here?"

I nearly jumped at the sound of his voice directly beside me. Damon was towering over me, those nearly turquoise eyes of his regarding me with interest.

He was the definition of intimidating, but I refused to bend my neck to him. Not after everything that happened.

"Lucifer, hi. It's been a while."

The receptionist's eyes bulged like she was expecting Damon to throttle me. All he did was look slowly down from my eyes to my chest and back up again with the faintest shadow of a smile.

The silence was broken by the receptionist. "She's here to interview, but Jason called out this morning. I was telling her she'd need to reschedule."

Damon started walking, then paused after a few steps and half turned. "Are you coming or not, Tinkerbell?"

He still remembered that stupid nickname?

Now the receptionist wasn't trying to hide the awe in her face. It was like I'd grown an angel halo and wings. I had to fight the urge to wink at her before scurrying after Damon.

He was already in the elevator when I reached him. He tapped the button for the top floor and waited.

Don't say thank you. Don't even acknowledge his vileness. Just stand here and let this play out, because you need the money, but you also don't need to show gratitude to the devil himself.

"Thanks," I said quietly. *Damn it, Chelsea.*

He stood silently until the elevator let us out on the top floor. "There's a conference room nobody uses on the next floor. Did you come for round two?"

I looked at him in disgust. "You think I'd go to the trouble of setting up an interview again just to sleep with you?"

He shrugged. "I don't really know the first thing about you. I have no idea what you would or wouldn't do."

"Then know this."

I paused when the elevator doors opened and a couple of young women filed in, but not before giving Damon a pair of salacious looks. I had to lower my voice and lean in toward him to finish my thought.

"I'm never letting *that* happen again. And I scheduled an interview here because it's the last agency I haven't applied to. Shockingly, I hoped to avoid working for you."

"I see."

I balled my fists at my side. That was all? *I see?* In a split second, I felt all the frustration and rage I felt toward Damon boil over in a blinding flash. I spun and punched his arm as hard as I could.

The two women behind us gasped, putting their hands to their mouths. Damon looked down at the spot I'd hit him and then took me by the wrist. The doors opened a moment later and he walked me out with him, then spun me against the wall.

There was rage in his eyes, but something else, too. "Nobody touches me. Nobody fucking *punches* me. Especially not in front of my employees."

"Those were your employees? They looked like they were former fuckbuddies from the way they were eyeballing you."

The nostrils on his annoyingly perfect nose flared. "Tell me, Tinkerbell. Why do you think you would be a good fit here at Rose?"

"You tested the fit five years ago and didn't have any complaints."

There was a pause, then the hint of a smile. "Funny. So your contribution to my company would be a childish sense of humor? Thanks, but I'll pass."

"My contribution would be that I wouldn't just tell you 'yes.'" I gestured to a pair of men who walked by with their heads bent and their eyes down as they passed us. It was a guess, but I had a feeling it was one with a fair shot at being dead on. "You're trying to run a company but everybody who works for you is too busy ducking their heads and avoiding eye contact, right? I've already shown you I'll stare you in the eye and speak my mind. You need someone like me."

Damon finally took a step back, making me feel like I could breathe again. He planted his hands on his hips, then scratched at the stubble on his chin, sizing me up. "Let me make something clear. I don't need anyone. *Nothing.* Least of all someone like you. Look around you. All of this is mine. My fucking empire. But I'd very much enjoy watching you try to survive in my world." He took a step toward me and tugged at the material of my shirt with his fingertips. "But when you show up for work tomorrow, try to wear something more presentable."

I thought about presenting him with two middle fingers, or maybe my foot between his legs. Instead, I giddily danced inside because I'd landed the job.

It had taken a bizarre streak of luck and circumstance for it to happen, but it was mine. I may not know *what* the job was, exactly, or what it paid. All I knew was Damon Rose challenged me once and I failed. This time, it was going to be different.

This time I was going to prove he had underestimated me. And maybe, just *maybe,* I'd get a chance to find out what kind of man the father of my child really was.

5

DAMON

Behind me, huge paneled windows lined my office wall. I had a clear view of the rectangular slice of green Central Park cut through New York City. Buildings like my own shot up around the edges. People I'd never meet hurried from place to place hundreds of feet below.

It made me think about something I'd heard before: imagine how dumb the average person is, then realize that means half of the world is dumber than that. I peeled myself from my thoughts to look at my brother, who might well reside in that lower half.

Chris sat across from me in my office with his fingers templed below his chin, as if he was contemplating some genius level topic in his mind.

"What?" I didn't bother to hide the irritation I felt. I was trying to figure out a PR scandal one of my basketball players had ignited in the middle of the night, and I wasn't in the mood to deal with my brother's shit.

"I'm just trying to figure out who the hell came up with sausages and hot dogs. Like... Who opens up an animal, sees intestines, and says, 'you know what would be delicious? Let's grind up this animal and stuff it inside its own intestines!'"

I sighed. "Is there anything else?"

"Yeah. Fish eggs. Like who in their right mind—"

"I've got a lot to work on, Chris. Unless there's something more pressing, it can wait."

He popped up to his feet and stopped at my door. "There is one thing. Coach might've said something about how if I don't find a way to focus more on the team and less on women, he wasn't going to renew my contract no matter how many touchdowns I throw this season." My brother shrugged, as if he hadn't just casually let me know Rose Athletic Representatives most lucrative athlete might be out of the job soon.

I stared. "He what? That's ridiculous. Why would he care what you do with women if you're performing on the field?"

My brother winced a little, then smirked. "There have been a few incidents. I didn't want to bother you with them since the team decided it was in everyone's best interest to keep them under wraps."

"Incidents?"

"You know, you're busy. We can talk about this later. Gotta jam!" Chris paused at the door. "You ever wonder why the phrase isn't, 'gotta jelly?' Or why a condiment in the first place. Actually, if you were going to go the condiment route, I feel like saying 'gotta ketchup' would make the most sense."

"Please," I groaned. "Go. And don't cause any more problems until I figure out how to fix this one."

Like a kid who knew he'd pissed off his parents and was glad to get off with a slap on the wrist, Chris slid wordlessly out the door and closed it, leaving me with a wonderful little ball of pressure in the back of my head with his name on it.

I was just getting my focus back when my office phone chimed. "Mr. Rose, there's a woman here who says you gave her a job yesterday. Should I call security?"

I grinned at that thought. It would be amusing to have security escort Chelsea out and pretend I'd never hired her. It would also mean she'd be gone for good this time. Which... was what I wanted, wasn't it?

"No." I tapped my finger on the desk. I hadn't even decided which circle of hell to send my little Tinkerbell to. Exile was too easy. I could condemn her to the mail room or HR. Or... "Send her to my office."

There was a long pause. "Your office, sir?"

"If the phones aren't clear enough to stop me from repeating myself, then call fucking IT." I shut off the call and rocked back in my chair, glaring at nothing in particular. Once upon a time, being an asshole had been a choice. When did it become so automatic?

It wasn't something I could afford to worry about. Trish had made sure of that. Leading by fear meant the ones planning to stab you in the back were easier to spot. If you treat everyone like equals and friends, the knife will come with a smile. Lead with fear, and you either got bent necks or hatred. I was happy to bend every neck under me and dispatch the ones dumb enough to glare back. It was ruthless, but effective.

It also meant I didn't make the same mistakes again—like trusting someone with my feelings or giving them the keys to hurt me. No. I'd learned the most important lesson from my ex, Trish. If you never let anyone in, you were fucking untouchable.

Tinkerbell was about to get a lesson in exactly what happened to people who had the nerve to defy me, and I was going to enjoy it.

My door opened a few minutes later. She walked in wearing another outfit that looked like it was plucked from the bargain bin of a thrift store—a dull skirt that stopped just above her knees and a tan, silky top that made her look like she belonged in an 80s law drama. I was only surprised it didn't have shoulder pads.

"Sit."

She waited just long enough to remind me she was a pain in my ass, then took the seat across from my desk. She sat with her thighs pressed together, but not so tightly that I couldn't get a generous glimpse of her smooth legs. A vivid memory of spinning her around and fucking her from behind assaulted my senses. With an effort, I pushed it down.

The years had been kind to Chelsea. She'd blossomed from what I assumed was her early twenties and the look of a girl just barely out of college to a woman. A full blown, obnoxiously attractive woman. She still had that slightly crooked, freckled nose. She didn't look as tan as I remembered, but her hips appeared wider and I even thought her chest had grown somewhat. Back then, she'd been hard, like an athlete at the peak of her career. Now she'd softened around the edges, and I couldn't help wondering how soft and delicious it'd feel to pull her body against mine.

Except those were thoughts I couldn't indulge.

There was absolutely not going to be a repeat of that encounter. She was at my company now, and the company was my life. I'd cut my own arm off before I risked it for a woman.

"Where will I be working?"

"Under me." I was speaking without thinking. *Under me? No. Send her to HR. To the front desk. Your dumbass doesn't need to be tempted by seeing her every single day.* I could already feel the foundations trembling. Somehow, some way, I was going to regret this. I knew it. "You'll be my personal assistant. Coffee runs, printing, faxing, deliveries, dry cleaning, and anything else I decide I can use you for."

Idiot.

She hesitated. "Anything else?"

I decided not to acknowledge the shared secret between us and how it might have colored my words. "Anything."

"And what will I be paid for this work?"

It was tempting to insult her with a low offer. Ten grand a year, for example. But I realized it'd be more satisfying to make the offer as juicy as I could. Because I was going to test her patience more than it had ever been tested, and the harder I made it to walk away, the more fun I could have. "Three hundred thousand a year. Full benefits."

To her credit, she kept a straight face, but her leg started shaking a few seconds later. "I assume I'll get that in writing?" Chelsea was speaking slowly with a controlled edge to her voice.

"You'll get what you get," I snapped.

"I want it in writing. A contract."

I had to take deep breaths. I'd obviously intended to give her one, but I bristled at having her *demand* it from me. "Fine. Your first task is to walk your ass down to HR and tell them to draft it up. They can call my office if they need confirmation. Happy?"

The stony look she'd been wearing since she walked in finally cracked. She jumped up from her chair, rushed over to me, and gave me a tight hug while jumping up and down giddily. "Thank you so much," she whispered. Then she rushed out of my office, leaving me to stare at the wall with the most confused erection of my life.

As if he could have worse timing, my brother stuck his head in my office a moment later. Annoyed, I put my hands in my lap. "Yes?"

"Look. I don't know how to say this, so I'm just going to try my best."

My heartbeat quickened. "What is it?"

"Worchestershire. Worsher? Worchester sauce? Fuck. See what I mean?"

"Get out of my office."

"Well, there's none in your so-called break room. I can't eat spaghetti and meatballs without a dab of it. So what do you expect me to do, exactly?"

With my brother, sometimes the only thing to do was wait

quietly until he lost interest. So I looked down at my computer and waited until I heard the door close.

Idiots. I was surrounded by idiots.

6

CHELSEA

I made my way to HR while *I'm a Bitch, I'm a Boss* played in my mental stereo system.

Three hundred thousand dollars a year. Full benefits.

Hell. Yes.

I ran through the things I could do with that kind of cold hard cash. It was like playing that game where you thought about what you'd do if you won the lottery. A new bra. A nice bra that fit right. Socks without holes my big toes poked through. New clothes for Luna instead of the second-hand stuff we had to settle for. Some real food for my brother.

And bills. *God.* I could slap my bills around like they were my bitch with that kind of money.

Still, I had to be careful not to go into full blown celebration mode. I'd need to reserve the double birds aimed at the sky and maniacal laughter until the check actually cleared. No matter how much I wanted to believe it, I had to remember who we were talking about here.

Damon Rose. He was the dickbreathed, cockfaced, assheaded guy who was luring me into his trap with piles and piles of money. It was either a trick to break my heart when he pulled it away at the last minute, or it was a sign that I was in for far worse than I could imagine. If he really planned to give me that money, he was challenging me, and I had a feeling the challenge was to find out what I'd put up with before I'd quit. He was just sadistic enough to do something like that, and I knew it.

I had to wait while the guy at HR called to confirm the details of my salary and position, but within an hour, I was signing my name at the bottom of a spicy contract that would take me straight from the ramen noodle diet to the name brand pasta diet. Yeah. You bet your ass Luna and I were going to be celebrating with some fancy pasta tonight. Fettuccine? Those little ones that look like helmets? The harder it was to spell, the more likely we were to buy it. It was going to be *that* kind of fancy. I might not even bring my coupon book to the grocery store just to flex a little bit.

I was leaving HR with a giant smile on my face when a young woman with red hair and tired eyes stopped me. She was breathtaking, even though she looked like she'd rather be punching puppies than at work. "Hey," she said dryly.

"Hi, I'm Chelsea."

"Daria."

I stuck out my hand for a handshake. She looked down at it, then grinned crookedly, taking it and giving it a quick shake. She looked over her shoulder, then stepped a little closer. I noticed she had the most gorgeous dark blue eyes and skin so perfect I couldn't help being jealous. "Damon is fucking obsessed with the color yellow."

I crinkled my nose. "What? I was just in his office and didn't see anything yellow."

"He doesn't like people to know. But if you wear yellow, he's always nicer."

"Oh, wow. Really?"

Daria nodded, then shot me a thumbs up. "You're welcome."

I smiled and waved goodbye to her. Apparently, part of my giant new salary was going to go toward adding a little yellow to my wardrobe.

Luna sat across from me that night with red sauce covering her face and a satisfied, tired look in her eyes. I'd invited Grant over as well as my best friend since high school, Milly.

Milly wore round, Harry Potter style glasses that I always found cute on her petite face and frame. Her brown hair was pulled back in a double braid that fell to her back, and she was dressed like she'd just gotten off the tennis court. Unlike me, Milly's tennis career hadn't come to an abrupt halt when she got pregnant. More accurately, Milly hadn't been careless and irresponsible enough to *get* pregnant. But that was always a strange thing to think about.

I hated that I was dumb enough to let it happen to me, but if you gave me a time machine and sent me back ten years, I'd agonize over how to make sure everything happened exactly the way it did because I'd lose my mind if Luna never happened. Go figure.

Milly was still clawing and fighting to get high enough in the rankings to earn a decent living, but at least she was out there.

Grant was unusually quiet, so I tossed a piece of the crust of my garlic bread at him. He grinned distractedly.

"Okay. Spit it out," I said.

On cue, Luna spit a mouthful of chewed up spaghetti onto her plate and grinned like a lunatic. We all let out a collective groan.

"Follow the rules for once," Luna said cheerily, reminding me of a talk we'd just had yesterday after I spoke with her pre-K teacher.

Grant shifted in his chair, then leaned in on his elbows. "This salary he's offering you. You've really got it in writing? I mean, like when does your first check come?"

"At the end of my second week."

"So what happens if he fires you before then?"

To tell the truth, I hadn't considered that. I'd been riding too high on the sudden weight of poverty getting yanked off my shoulders. "Why would I get fired?"

Milly cleared her throat. "Obvious historical complications between you and Lucifer?"

"Who's Lucifer?" Luna asked.

Milly smirked. "Your mommy is Lucifer when she hasn't had her coffee."

I could see the gears in Luna's little head turning, and knew I was going to get woken up tomorrow morning by my little girl calling me the devil. *Thanks, Milly.*

"None of that matters," I said. "I need the money, so I'll play nice."

"It doesn't strike you as odd that he's offering you such an insane salary to be his personal assistant?" Milly asked.

"It's a little strange, yeah. But he's loaded. Maybe he just pulled a number out of his grumpy butt." Of course, I'd already speculated on his motivations and decided he was trying to screw me, either figuratively or literally. I didn't feel like admitting that to Milly and my brother, though.

Luna giggled with joy to hear me drop the "B" word. I gave her a little conspiratorial wink.

Milly shook her head. "Rich people are obsessed with money. It makes them even cheaper. I think he is playing some sort of game with you. He offers you an insane amount of money so he can take more pleasure in tormenting you into quitting. The money is just there to buy him time before you get fed up and walk out."

"There's literally nothing he could do to make me walk away

from three hundred thousand dollars a year. I mean, *almost* nothing."

Milly waved her fork toward my brother. "Grant, help me out here."

He was studying the table. "It's a lot of money. *A lot.* You could change a lot of lives with that kind of cash."

"See?"

Milly let out a dejected sigh. "Fine. You can walk into this whole thing blind and ignorant, but don't come crying to me when he breaks your heart into a million pieces and you wind up quitting."

"My *heart*? Oh, no, no. My heart has nothing to do with this at all. I'll be leaving that at home, thank you very much."

"Famous last words."

I stuck my tongue out. "Roast chicken. There. Now those weren't my last words."

"As always," Milly said. "You're a beacon of maturity and wisdom."

I smiled to myself, but my thoughts were wandering. I'd already decided Damon was trying to trap me somehow. But what if it wasn't just about proving a point?

As much as I might talk a big game about leaving my heart out of the equation, I knew one thing: Damon was Luna's father. He might be the devil incarnate and I could hate that it had to be him and not the guy of my dreams, but… There would always be a part of me that longed to give Luna her father. I wished I could make that part of her life complete, but the Damon I knew was too heartless to be in her life.

Men disappointed. They promised things and took them away. They let you down. They only wanted sex, and then once you'd given it up, they disappeared. At least Damon had made the sex enjoyable.

No. Bad. You do not need to be making a pros and cons list. You shouldn't even be considering whatever it is you're considering.

I could point to the money or the opportunity all I wanted, yet there was part of me that wondered if what really had my hopes up was the chance to find out if there was anything worth saving in him.

I never claimed to be a smart woman.

7

DAMON

Chris sat across from me at a posh restaurant downtown. It was the sort of place where every dish came with a "story" and illustrated some moment of the chef's childhood. Personally, I preferred to keep my food simple, and this sort of place drove me up the wall. My brother loved it.

It also meant the servers spent way too damn long droning on at the table. Tonight, our waitress was a young, pretty brunette who couldn't seem to decide if she wanted to eye fuck me or Chris more. He was eating it up, of course, and I wished she'd just leave us to eat our ridiculous, edible flowers and sugar-glass bubbles, or whatever shit my brother ordered.

He smacked his lips theatrically, then pointed to his plate. "Seriously. It's like you can picture Chef Torrone under the table while his grandma was making bread. I can almost see the flour drifting down around him."

"That's wonderful. Now that your stomach is full, can we discuss this properly?"

My brother lifted his napkin to wipe at his already-clean mouth. "If we must."

"You've become a liability to your sponsors. I'm getting calls every day. They're threatening to pull their deals with us."

"Then we get new ones."

"These *are* the new ones. You can only screw up so many times before you run out of options, Chris. Either you shape up and start at least playing by some of the rules, or you'll lose them all."

"I like women. I like to party. I fail to see how that separates me from every other professional athlete with shoe deals and TV spots."

"Most recently? You liked a woman in a public park in full view of paparazzi. If we want to dig into history, like, say, a month ago? Then you also partied with certain illegal substances while cameras were rolling during an award ceremony. Do I need to continue, or is my point setting in?"

"You have to ask that often, don't you?"

"What?"

He smirked. "Is your point in yet? When it's so small, you've probably got to double check with them."

"Could you at least pretend to take this seriously? We're talking about millions of dollars on the line. In case you forgot, that matters to both of us."

"What are you proposing, exactly? Some sort of celibacy stunt? Like I go two weeks without fucking?"

"I don't know yet, but we're going to need to come up with something."

"Hey," Chris pointed past me. "Isn't that your little friend?"

I spotted Chelsea at the entrance of the restaurant. She was trying to explain something to the hostess while gesturing in my direction. The hostess looked toward me, then sent a young man in a suit to talk to me.

"I'm sorry to interrupt you, sirs. That young woman claims there's something she needs to give you."

I hid the smile I felt threatening to come. I shook my head.

"I've never seen her in my life. Please make sure she doesn't bother us."

The man nodded, then went back to the hostess, who said a few clipped words to Chelsea. I only had time to see her shoot me a glare of pure ice before she was escorted out of the building.

"What was that about?" Chris asked.

"I told her to meet me here."

He shifted his eyes to the side. "Right. And then you had her removed from the building? Any reason in particular you're tormenting the girl?"

"None that should worry you."

"Well, at least you're showing an interest in something other than counting money. I guess I should be happy."

"I'm not showing an interest. I'm making a point."

"If the point is that you're an asshole, then trust me, there's no need to go to all the effort."

"As much fun as this is, I'm going to head back to the office. One of us has work to do."

Chris reached across the table and pulled my mostly untouched plate to his side. "I only let you believe I don't bust my ass. It's part of my charming image. As soon as you're not watching, I'll be working, too. On this French model. She doesn't even shave her legs. It's very exotic. Scratchy, but exotic."

"Charming. Right. Do me a favor and focus on having a personality that doesn't cost me millions of dollars for a change."

"Yeah, well, gotta spend money to make it. Right?"

"No. Not in this context. Just, no."

I WASN'T PREPARED TO ADMIT IT—EVEN UNDER TORTURE—BUT I was looking forward to seeing how Chelsea planned to handle the first hurdle I'd laid out for her. Nobody made eye contact with me as I entered the company building through the lobby and headed toward the elevators. They all knew better by now, I supposed.

My thoughts were still on my brother's situation. Chris was the foundation that made everything I did easier. With him, all we had to do to snap up new clients was point to Chris. Had it not been for Trish and her catastrophic exit from Rose Athletic Representatives *and* my life, I wouldn't have felt so reliant on my brother. Instead, he was the biggest name we had left by far, and without him, I didn't know what our future would hold.

As his brother, I wanted to help him right the course before it was too late. At the CEO of a multi-million-dollar business, I needed to make sure I had a backup plan.

In other words, I needed to find someone remotely comparable to Chris' star power to bring on.

I was meeting with Tia Klein this afternoon, the up-and-coming golfer slash Instagram influencer. She was apparently above average on the course, if not quite a top tier pro. But she also had millions who clung to her every word about makeup products and fashion online. She wouldn't be a Chris Rose, but I had to test all my options. Maybe someone who had proven they knew how to leverage their looks and position to carve out a social media following would be a good start. A new breed of client, even.

When I reached my floor, I found a small gathering of people near the break room. Men and women were crowded around outside trying to arch their necks to look inside. Once they saw me coming, it was like Moses and the Red Sea parting.

Excited murmuring turned to hushed whispers as those who had spotted me scrambled to their desks to pretend they were working.

Inside the break room, I found Chelsea and Tia Klein talking as casually as old friends.

I frowned. "Tia. I wasn't expecting you for a few hours."

"Scheduling conflict," she said, waving her hand dismissively. "I was just letting your personal assistant know about it."

"Right. Well, I can see you now, if that's what this is about."

More of my employees were doing the wise thing and inching their way out of the room by the second. Still, I could feel the presence of the nosiest ones lingering to listen behind me.

Tia had silky black hair and a firm athlete's body. She might've passed for gorgeous to some, but I found her supreme air of confidence to be more of the holier than thou brand, which put me off her immediately. She had exotic features that made her appear almost cat-like—a feature she seemed to emphasize on purpose from the way she swayed as she crossed the room toward me.

"Chelsea was telling me how close you two are."

I felt my stomach clench. She was *what?* "Did she tell you anything else?" I asked carefully.

Chelsea looked at me in a way that made me positive I was going to want to strangle her in a few seconds. "I was just saying how you've been so kind to me. Really the best boss I could've hoped for."

I manufactured my best smile. "Right. I'm glad you're enjoying it here."

"Well," Tia said. "I was hoping I could move our meeting to tonight. I've got a fundraiser thing at my place. Maybe you could come and we could get a few drinks in us before we talk boring business? And bring this girl." She gave a little tilt of her head toward Chelsea. "I like her."

Once Tia was gone, I pushed every lingering employee out of the break room and closed the doors. I turned to face Chelsea, who had her back to the counter.

"She was nice," Chelsea said.

"What was that?"

"Leverage?"

"Tell me why I shouldn't just fire you on the spot for fucking with a client of mine? Telling her how *close* we were? It couldn't be farther from the truth. And I don't want you talking to potential clients or existing clients without my express permission. God knows what you could screw up if you say the wrong thing."

"You shouldn't fire me on the spot because you want to chase me away. You think I won't be able to handle the punches you're going to throw, and you want to watch me walk away with my tail between my legs. You won't fire me because that's not how you decided this was going to go, and you're too stubborn to change your mind on that."

Truth be told, I was currently remembering when *I* was between her legs. She looked even better after five years apart. She was full figured, wild-eyed, and I still hadn't been able to forget how it'd felt to be inside her.

She'd been haunting me for five years, and now she was here. *In the flesh.*

"Let me guess, this time will be different?" I was talking about our little bet five years ago—when I'd told her I could make her say "yes" and she didn't believe it. We'd pitted our wills against each other before, and I'd come out on top in more ways than one. Now she seemed to think it was going to be different. Of course, I did have *some* semblance of professionalism, and I wasn't going to spell that out for her.

"This may be a game to you, but it's an opportunity for me. Did I tell her we were close? Yes. And now you're inclined to bring me to an important meeting with an important client. You think I'm going to quit, but I'm going to show you exactly why you need me here."

I folded my arms. "I need you? Do you even know the first thing about athletic agencies? Representing clients? Structuring contracts?"

"If you figured it out, I'm sure I can."

"If you last long enough. I'll see you at the fundraiser. Try to dress nice for a change."

8
CHELSEA

I put my hands on my knees, drumming my fingers awkwardly. The nightlife of New York City was crawling by the car window as we inched through traffic. I was also sitting next to an old man I'd never met. Apparently, his name was "Dick," and he'd been sent by Damon to drive me to the fundraiser.

Dick wore a felt hat with a stubby brim over his age speckled head. He had a long, hook nose, teeth so perfect I suspected they were dentures, and he was dressed in an adorable little cardigan.

"So..." I said after a few minutes of quiet. "Do you usually drive people around for Damon?"

"Usually? I rub his feet. Oil him down before photoshoots. Sometimes I'll massage the little knot he gets out of his ass cheek."

I stared.

Dick waited a long few seconds before he grinned. "Those were supposed to be jokes. It'll be less uncomfortable for both of us if you laugh when I try to be funny."

I found myself smiling with him. "Sorry. Everything has been so crazy since I took the job for Damon. I'm having trouble keeping up."

Dick nodded. "I can relate. I was there myself when he took me on."

"I've always wondered," I said suddenly. "How do you get Dick from Richard, anyway?"

"Oh, it's easy. Just buy me dinner."

I spurted out a surprised laugh, then tried to compose myself.

"So," Dick said, shifting his eyes my way. "What's with all the yellow?"

I self-consciously looked down at my outfit. Okay. It was possible that I took Daria's advice a little too far when I got myself ready tonight. Almost every article of clothing and jewelry I had on was at least a little yellow.

"It was just what I threw on," I lied.

"You look like the man in the yellow hat from Curious George. Minus the hat, the dick, and with a pair of knockers."

I let out a sigh and stared out the window. "Someone told me Damon likes yellow. I wanted him to be a little nicer to me for a change."

Dick let out a hacking laugh. "Someone was fucking with you."

"What?"

"He hates yellow. Rumor is he fired a guy for wearing a yellow tie once. Went on some long tirade about how only a tasteless, half blind idiot would wear a yellow tie to work."

I swallowed.

DEAR DARIA,
You suck.
Sincerely,
Me

I ARRIVED AT THE FUNDRAISER IN ONE PIECE, THANKED DICK—THE

driver, not the anatomy that had gotten me into this mess in the first place—and headed inside.

I mostly ignored the fancy decorations, swarms of attractive, well-dressed people, and headed straight for the bar. I figured I could probably sneak in a pleasant buzz before Damon found me, and God knew I needed a little liquid courage to get through this event without trying to strangle him.

Halfway through my second drink, a guy about my age with an English accent leaned in towards my ear. "Unbelievable, isn't it?"

I smiled politely, which was the universal signal for not being witty or with-it enough to figure out what he was talking about. I hoped he wasn't going to bring up my outfit.

"These people," he continued without missing a beat. "They prance around like it's all some sort of competition. Bet you ask half of them what cause we're raising money for and they'd have no idea."

I smiled again, or more like cringed. I was that half of people he was talking about. "Clueless. All of them."

He tipped his glass toward me and clinked it against mine. "You said it."

I cleared my throat, surveying the room. "You come to these things often?"

"I'm Mace. I'm an agent and I represent some of the athletes here."

"Mace? Like the anti-perv spray or the medieval weapon?"

He smiled crookedly. "Like my parents picked my name from a book of 'cool' baby names for boys."

Within a few minutes, Mace and I were smiling and laughing about a story involving one of his soccer players and a stolen mascot's mask from an opposing team. That was precisely when Lucifer shat all over what was shaping up to be an enjoyable night.

"Mace," Damon said. I was reminded of how tall and

imposing he was. Until Damon had arrived, I would've classified Mace as a big man. He was strong and tall, but Damon made him look smaller. "That's my personal assistant, so, if you don't mind."

Mace crooked an eyebrow. "Your employees aren't allowed to socialize at social events? I'd heard you run a crooked ship, but that's low. Even for you."

"I don't want you trying to fuck my employees. She has the best healthcare money can buy, but I'd rather not have my staff riddled with your STD's."

Mace snorted. "You're just as charming as always, Damon."

Damon signaled the bartender for a drink. "You should ignore everything he says, Chelsea. This man is a snake, and he'll bend you backwards and fuck you dry if you let him."

I snorted into my glass. "Sounds like someone else I know."

Damon choked on his liquor and had to wipe his mouth with the back of his hand. My little quip had Mace's eyebrows nearly above his hairline. "You two..."

"No." Damon snapped.

"Are you still—"

"Stay away from her."

Mace and I both gave Damon curious looks.

He seemed to bristle. "I don't need outside agencies fucking with my employees. That's all."

Mace wore a grin that didn't seem quite as kind as the ones he'd given me. "I would expect a man with your reputation to have thicker skin. She happened years ago, but you're still cowering from the memory of it, aren't you?"

"You can leave now."

"I was invited, asshole." Mace smiled at me a little sadly. "Good luck with him. And he *does* bite. Keep your distance."

"I can handle him. Thanks, though."

Damon made an annoyed sound and then gestured for me to follow.

"Grandpa Dick. Really?" I asked once we passed out of the

main lobby area and into a smaller, less crowded side room. What I really wanted to ask about was the mystery woman Mace had mentioned, but Damon was pissed enough that I knew he wouldn't answer.

Couches lined the walls and a few quiet groups of well-dressed individuals sat with drinks and cocktails.

Damon ran his tongue across his teeth in a way I thought might be meant to mask a smile. "He has been with the company for a long time. You made it here in one piece, didn't you?"

Chris shouldered his way through the crowd and tapped Damon on the shoulder. "Hey, did you know she-who-must-not-be-named is here? Want me to sneak you out the back?"

Damon's expression darkened. He shook his head. "No."

"What about that thing you said?" Chris lowered his voice, doing his best Damon impression. "If I have to set eyes on that woman again, I'll throw up so hard you'll have to push my feet back in my mouth."

"I'm nearly certain I never said that." Damon crossed his arms, eyes scanning the room. "And no. I'm not going anywhere."

Chris shrugged. "Fine with me. I did my brotherly duty, now it's on you." With that, he headed back where he'd come from, leaving Damon and I alone again.

"Who is 'she?'"

"Nobody you need to worry about."

I admittedly wanted to argue with him. I wanted to bug him until he gave me every delicious little detail of whatever drama he and his brother had just skirted around. Part of me *liked* the friction between us. I guessed if all you ever had was peace, it would be hard to appreciate the quiet moments when they came. God knew there was no peace around my bosshole, Damon.

I followed Damon to one of the couches in the back, where Tia Klein was lounging with a heavily tattooed young man I took to be another athlete.

"Is now a good time?" Damon asked.

Tia shooed the guy away and gestured for us both to sit. I was struck by how catlike she was. Graceful and dangerous. Then again, for graceful creatures, cats really had a way of sticking that one leg up in the air and going to town on their own buttholes when it suited them. I grinned at the idea of Tia Klein—Little Miss Put Together and exotic beauty queen of Instagram—grooming herself noisily. Then I cringed.

Ew.

Tia and Damon launched into some boring talk about business and contracts while I tried to get that image out of my head. The topic of their conversation shifted and drew me back into focus.

"...Made the mistake of fucking you first, didn't she?"

Damon visibly stiffened, then shot a sideways glance my way. "I'd prefer not to talk about my personal life in front of my employees."

A dangerous glint entered Tia's eyes as she moved her focus to me. "Damon is quite the playboy. Did you know? Except he has never let me into his bedroom. I guess I'm not sexy enough for the legendary Damon Rose and his magical cock."

I raised my eyebrows. "Magical cock, huh? What does it do, activate its shrinking powers when anyone else is in the room?"

Tia cackled with delight. "I really like this one, Damon. You need to keep her around. It'll be good for that inflated ego of yours."

"You haven't given me an answer," Damon said sternly. "Do you want to stop letting a hack represent you? He's happy to let the contracts you were already going to get keep coming and continue to take his cut. Sign with me, and I'll turn you into a brand. I'll get you sponsorships and deals you didn't even know were out there."

"Of course I'm going to sign with you. Who turns down Damon Rose?"

I wanted to barf. Even with the teasing, Tia was making no

secret of the fact that she wanted to sleep with Damon. She was practically purring the words while she undressed him with her eyes. To his credit, he was laser focused on the business aspect of the deal, at least for now. I wondered if the man who was willing to sleep with me five years ago after a few seconds of introduction was really going to refrain from sticking his dick in a client for long, though.

Then I remembered I didn't need to care. Damon could take his "magical" pecker and stick it in a light socket for all I cared.

I was only here for the money. Not even a single part of this whole fiasco was about trying to give him a chance to prove he deserved to know he had a daughter.

Not even a little bit.

But... If I had to sit and watch Tia slather herself all over him for another minute, I thought I might end up tossing my water on her face. To make matters worse, Damon wasn't exactly beating her away with a stick. He just sat there, letting her flirt.

Yeah. It was time for a bathroom break. The kind of bathroom break that takes a long detour to the bar. I doubted he'd even notice I was gone with Tia's Instagram-perfect tits in his face.

9
DAMON

This sort of thing made me want to find the nearest beach and start kicking down sandcastles. *Fuck.* Fundraisers in general weren't the problem. Rich assholes like myself *should* open up their wallets and give back. The problem was nobody here cared about the cause. It was all about status and power.

From the top to the bottom, it was a pissing contest, and I was obligated to produce the largest stream to make a good show for Rose Athletic Representatives.

Yoo goddamn hoo.

Part of my image was being the best. I was the Rolls Royce of athletic representation, so I had to make sure I showed I wasn't shy about throwing money around. That meant I was seated closest to the stage beside Tia Klein herself. I'd also paid enough that Chris, his date, and Chelsea had places at the table. It was all an extravagance, but a necessary one.

The dining hall buzzed with conversation as we took our seats and dishes started to be served. Normally, I would've gotten up from my seat and circulated the room, doing my best to shake the right hands and make sure athletes I had my eye on knew who I was and where to find me.

Tonight, I didn't have the stomach for it. Chelsea had worn the most godawful assortment of clothing I think any woman had ever put on. Yellow. Every single thread was yellow.

Ever since I was a kid, I'd had a particular dislike of the color. And yes, the rumors were mostly true. I had fired *Todd* and his stupid named self from my office for wearing a yellow tie. The part nobody got right in the story was that Todd also had mustard smeared in his patchy mustache from his lunch. Dried, crusty, mustard. It made me physically sick to look at, and I fired him by reflex.

Knowing Chelsea, someone had tipped her off to the fact that I hated yellow and put her up to this. But I was a grown ass man. It was just a color. I'd survive the night, even if I would need to avert my eyes from the fluorescent blob that was my personal assistant.

Tia sat to my right, where she was busy trying to snap the perfect selfie for her Instagram account. Chelsea was to my left and somehow engaged in animated discussion with Chris' date, who looked like her brain might've fit in a peanut shell.

Was there anyone this woman couldn't get along with?

Yeah, *me*. We butted heads every time we were together, and when we weren't fighting, we were fucking. What a beautiful relationship.

"Would it kill you to stay focused?" I said quietly in her ear, cutting her off mid-sentence.

"I'm so sorry, boss," Chelsea said sweetly. "I sometimes forget that you own me, and I'm not allowed to pee without your permission."

I knew she was only teasing, but even hearing her jokingly say I owned her made my skin prickle with heat. It brought up vivid flashbacks of my hand buried in her hair and her soft ass against my hips. "I need my personal assistant to act like she's here as an employee and not at a social event. And I need her to show she has some common sense the next time she gets dressed."

Chelsea's cheeks flushed. "Somebody misled me. *About the yellow*," she added in a near whisper.

I leaned closer. "What do you mean?"

Chelsea just shook her head. "I'm not going to tell you. It's too embarrassing. Can we just pretend I'm not wearing any of this?"

"No," I said, trying to expel the image of her stripped bare and naked. I did not need to picture that. "That wouldn't be a good idea."

Chelsea caught the look on my face, then grinned. "Like what you see, boss?" She wiggled her eyebrows.

"You said someone misled you. What did you mean?"

She sighed. "Daria said you love yellow. She said you're super nice to people when they wear yellow. Then Dick told me on the ride over about how you tore some poor guy's head off just for wearing a yellow tie. So..."

I cracked a smile. "You thought dressing as a lemon would get me to be nice to you?"

Chelsea glared.

"Did you ever consider not being a sarcastic, back-talking pain in my ass?"

"No. Wearing yellow sounded a lot less painful than having to kiss your ass. I was going to load my closet with fifty shades of yellow if that was what it took."

"You probably shouldn't trust Daria, by the way," I said.

"Yeah, no shit. Why would she try to trick me?"

"Daria has a twisted sense of humor. It's nothing personal, probably. She's... not amused by normal things."

"Well, I've got to use the restroom. Am I allowed to pee on the clock, boss?"

"I'd suggest the toilet."

She stared for a few seconds, then half-smiled. "Was that a joke?"

"No," I said sternly. "Now go use the bathroom."

She got up, glanced back at me once, then left.

"You two have an interesting relationship," Chris noted. "It sounds like you need to practice a little sexual therapy."

"Hardly."

I felt a hand slide across my thigh. Tia was smiling down at it. "If she's not willing, I'm sure someone else would spend the night with you."

I didn't quite understand why I felt so repulsed by the idea of sleeping with Tia. I still wanted her as a client, so I didn't quite rip her hand off my leg like I wanted to. Instead, I gave a tight smile. "Thanks, but I'll have to pass."

She tilted her head. "Saving yourself for the personal assistant, then?"

"I don't sleep with clients. And I don't sleep with employees."

"Then maybe I'll refuse to sign the contract until I've had a taste of Damon Rose and his magic cock?"

Chris laughed. "Only thing magic about Damon's cock is that it disappears after paying you a visit."

I decided to get up and go find Chelsea, because even her constant attitude was preferable to listening to my own brother talk about my penis.

I was stopped by a pair of basketball players, then an agent from a rival company, and finally one of the biggest shoe sponsors I worked with. By the time I detached myself from the conversations, Chelsea had been M.I.A. for over an hour. When I finally found her, she was at the bar again talking to Mace.

I gritted my teeth, then moved to her side. "Come on. You've had enough."

She swirled to look up at me and I realized she really had. It looked like she was well on her way to not remembering anything else about tonight.

"She's an adult," Mace said.

"An adult who has drank too much and needs to get home."

He grinned. "Since when do you give a shit about anyone other than yourself?"

"She's on my payroll. If she dies of alcohol poisoning, I'll end up having to talk to lawyers. I hate lawyers."

"Fuck you and your lawyers," Chelsea said. "I'll die if I want to, *bitch*."

I took her arm and tried to get her to stand, but she threw her face forward, head butting me in the stomach.

"What the hell?" I staggered back, not sure if I should laugh or start swearing.

"Come on, tough guy. You want me to come home with you, then learn to take a head butt like a man."

How much had she had to drink while she was gone? "Just get up and come outside with me. I'll get you a ride home."

"You just want to put that big, juicy cock in me again. Don't you?"

Mace's eyes went wide. The look on my face must've confirmed to him that she was telling the truth, because he went from looking shocked to contemplative a moment later.

"Get lost, Mace."

He stood, threw back the rest of his drink, and leaned into Chelsea's ear. "I enjoyed our conversation, sweetheart."

"Outside," I said.

"Yeah, yeah." Chelsea slurred. She had to lean on me to make it outside while remaining upright.

I called my driver while she hummed something tunelessly.

Chelsea rambled about anything that seemed to cross her mind on the drive home. She went from the best way to cook bacon—a griddle, apparently— to the fact that if you re-read Harry Potter and replace the word "wand" with "penis" it becomes the greatest fantasy comedy ever written.

She was staggering out of the car while mumbling, "Wizard's duel, Malfoy said. No contact. Penises only. Harry gripped his penis tight, eyes wide." She giggled madly but let me help her up the steps of the apartment.

I frowned when a thin man who looked around thirty answered the door. "Ah, shit," he said, taking her from me gently. "Too much to drink?"

"You are?" I asked. I barely controlled the rage I felt bubbling up. The moment I saw some guy open up the door to her place, I realized I didn't know Chelsea at all. That shouldn't have pissed me off, but it did. She'd been flirting with Mace at the bar while some guy waited at home for her? And what about me? Maybe we sparred, but—

Stop it, dumbass. You don't own her, and she doesn't owe you a thing.

"Her brother. You must be the asshole boss."

A small voice called out from deeper in the apartment, followed by tiny thumping footsteps. "Mommy!" A little girl with dark curls jumped up and latched onto Chelsea's leg like a baby monkey. "Who is he?" She asked, turning her attention to me.

Chelsea was a mother? I kept staring because the fact didn't want to settle in. She couldn't be a mother. She was too... Something. And who was the father? It felt like *my* head was spinning now.

Chelsea hugged the little girl back, looking a little more sober. "Mind if we stay over tonight, Grant?" She asked.

"Yeah, no worries." He looked up at me. "Uh, thanks for bringing her back."

"Make sure she remembers to show up to work tomorrow. *On time.*"

He regarded me quietly. "You really are an asshole, huh?"

I closed the door and headed back to the car.

She had a kid. I didn't know how that changed things, but it did. Maybe it should've made me feel more guilty about trying to terrorize her into quitting. Or maybe it should've made me feel like more of a creep for still revisiting the memory of what we'd done together five years ago.

Instead, I wanted answers. Who was the father, and why hadn't she told me she had a kid?

Because you're a monumental prickhead to her and she had no reason to tell you anything remotely personal?

I sighed. None of it mattered. I was forgetting what *really* mattered, like the fundraiser I'd paid a shitload of money to attend. The same one I'd walked away from without a moment's hesitation to bring my drunken personal assistant home.

I was losing my touch, and I needed to stop letting my games with Chelsea distract me from my business.

I was *not* going to let Chelsea become the next Trish. Not this time. Not again.

10

CHELSEA

Keys clattered, computers hummed, and the woman near my "desk" with the messy bob hairstyle crunched down her thousandth handful of peanuts in the last hour. Last Friday had been my first day, and this was officially the start of my first full week. When I came in this morning, I thought it was a Monday miracle to learn Damon had granted me with my own personal working space.

Then I'd been led to the dead center of the floor where a ridiculous little desk and stool sat. The other twenty or so men and women who worked on the floor had cubicles or elegant little partitions to give them some semblance of personal space. The girl who had shown me to my desk apologetically let me know that she was sure some kind of walls were probably going to be delivered soon.

I wasn't so sure. She hadn't sounded very confident, either.

I'd also been issued a company laptop, which I quickly learned was slow and a fire risk—namely because I wasn't sure if I could use it for an entire day without dumping a can of gasoline on it and lighting a match. The desktop wallpaper was plastered with a cheesy graphic that advised me to "Smile, because you're a Rose now!"

Barf.

My email inbox was graced with a request from Damon to organize every payment one of his athletes received in 2017 in descending order. He gave me a link to some sort of directory with all the information, which required me to dig through countless files.

I Facetimed Milly during my lunch break—which was a pack of peanut butter crackers I ate at my desk. Milly was rocking a healthy sweat and it looked like she was on some sort of beautiful rooftop tennis court. A pair of handsome guys were volleying in the background behind her while joking about something.

Milly squinted at the phone, leaning a little closer. "Wow. Where are you sitting? Why does it look like you're sitting in the middle of the room?"

I pulled a face. "Because I am."

"It's better than the utility closet though, right? Is he starting to like you?"

"Hardly. I think this is a punishment. I kinda got dirty drunk at the fundraiser. Grant said Damon personally dragged me to the door. That also means he probably saw Luna."

"You think he put two and two together?"

"No." Milly knew everything about me, including who Luna's father was. Even Grant didn't know that much, and he was nice enough not to pry about it. I lowered my voice a little, even though the majority of the office seemed to prefer to leave work to eat lunch. At least if you didn't count the peanut muncher from hell, that was. "He thinks he had a condom on, so why would he assume she was his?"

Milly worked her lips to the side, thinking. "Well, what did he say when you came in today?"

"Nothing. I got shown to my fancy new desk and he gave me an assignment that's going to keep me busy all freaking day."

"So he's mad at you."

"Then he should come say it to my face."

"Go to his office and ask him about it."

I popped a cracker in my mouth, then spoke with my mouth partially full. "You're right. I'm going to give him a piece of my mind."

"I'll be expecting the juicy details tonight." Milly shot me a thumbs up, then ended the call.

I set my phone down, dusted the crumbs off my hands, and headed for Damon's office.

I opened the door without knocking. His computer was partially visible, and I caught just enough of a glimpse to see him quickly close his internet browser. Before he closed it, I'd seen a picture of myself from my social media page where I was smiling into the camera beside Luna.

"What were you—"

"Knocking. Have you heard of it?"

"That was a picture of me."

"Congratulations. You can recognize your own face. Do you have any other special talents?"

"Don't try to bosshole this under the rug. What were you doing?"

Damon turned his chair to face me, then seemed to deflate a little. "Your daughter. I didn't expect that."

"And?"

"And you're my employee. Part of my job is to know my employees. I didn't want any more surprises."

"So you stalked my social media."

"Is her father still in the picture?"

"I'm not obligated to fill you in on my personal life. And the answer is complicated."

Damon nodded, then motioned to the chair across from his desk. "You can sit, if you like."

"Oh, I've had plenty of sitting for one day. My desk in the center of the office is really comfortable."

He looked like he was trying not to smile.

"It's a little sad, you realize that, right? The way you take so much joy in your childish little sleights."

"When I was a kid," Damon said. "I used to play this game with Skittles. I'd take out the whole bag and squish them together two at a time. One always squishes the other, while the other stays intact. I'd eat the squished one and test the intact Skittle against the next opponent. Eventually, I'd be left with the strongest Skittle in the bag. I'd save that one and pit it against the next bag I got. Eventually, I found one green Skittle that just wouldn't break. It tore through everything I threw at it. I became fascinated with trying to crack it. I stopped eating the squished ones and just started getting as many Skittles as I could get my hands on. But it never broke."

He stopped, as if that was the entire story. "So you were a psychopath when you were a little kid. Is that the moral of the story?"

"No. The moral of the story is that I eventually decided to just eat the green Skittle myself. In the world of Skittles, it was king. But in my world, it was just a snack."

I frowned at him. "Did you just call me a snack, Mr. Rose?"

If I didn't know better, I'd say his cheeks took on the faintest shade of red. "I'm..." He swallowed, then waved his hand. "Telling you to get back to work. I expect those figures by tonight. In ascending order. And alphabetized."

"Your email said descending. And how do I alphabetize a list of numbers, exactly?"

"Do what I say and get back to work, Miss Cross."

I stood. I was going to kill him. And if he thought he could just squish me until I broke like one of his stupid little Skittles, I'd teach him. And seriously, *Skittles?* Was a grown ass man really trying to threaten me by comparing me to candy?

11

DAMON

I only agreed to represent my brother as his agent when he got drafted into the NFL because I saw the vultures coming for him. All it took was a little research to see how common it was. A young athlete starts earning money, and everyone with even the most remote connection to them comes out of the woodwork to "help." Uncles, aunts, mothers, and fathers. It was always the same story. Someone with the supposed best interest of the athlete would step in with the goal of extracting as much of their hard-earned money as possible.

Did I profit from my brother's success? Yes. Greatly. But I made sure nothing I did ever jeopardized his future as an athlete. In fact, one of my biggest overriding goals for Chris was to create a brand for him that would continue to provide him with wealth long after he took his last snap in the NFL. It had been the drive behind my Olympic Games idea five years ago. That had fallen through, but I was still breaking boundaries with my representation of Chris.

When I branched out and started representing more athletes, I initially focused just on the ones I could tell were being preyed on by family members. Maybe you could call it a passion or a cause. Frankly, I didn't give a shit what you'd call it because I never spoke about it to a living soul. As far as anyone else knew, my solitary motivation for what I did was money, and they were welcome to keep believing that.

Life was easier when people didn't know the truth.

My company had grown, and I had to make decisions purely for profit more often than not. But I still picked up the occasional stray athlete that baffled my employees. They believed I was operating on some secret knowledge or potential. In reality, I wanted to save them. I saw little pieces of my brother in all of them, and I wanted to help protect them.

The more my business grew and the more financial resources we have, the better I could do that.

It was my secret because it had to be. If word got out that I took on charity cases, I'd never know who really needed help anymore. I'd be flooded by sob stories and pathetic young kids with tears in their eyes.

Even Chris didn't really know what drove me, and that was the way I wanted it to stay.

Chris slung his phone down on the couch in my office, groaning. "Fuck. I lost myself the playoffs in fantasy. That fumble in the third quarter last night was the deciding factor."

"You draft yourself on your own fantasy teams? Of course you do." I set down the stack of papers I was reviewing. It was yet another late night in my office. I had fires to put out, like usual.

I'd grown faster than I could keep up with, which meant hiring employees after my early days with Chris and the first few clients. Then it meant a building. Then an office downtown. Somewhere along the line, it turned into this. I sat at the top of a high rise building fixing problems caused by people who worked for me that I barely knew.

"I ate at this sushi place last night. They served squid that moved around when they poured sauce on it. You ever heard of that? I could swear I felt it moving in my stomach all night."

I grimaced. "Is there a reason you're in my office? I have actual work to do."

The door opened. It had to nearly be midnight, but Chelsea was still here, apparently. She stomped into my office with a stack of papers in her hand and flopped them down on my desk. "There. Everything you asked for."

"It took you that long?"

She looked like she was barely containing the urge to reach across the desk and throttle me. Her normally messy hair was wild, even by her standards. She'd clearly reached the point of running her hands through her hair in frustration at some point today and never looked back. Her blouse was half untucked from her skirt, and I was immediately met with the memory of how I'd been the one to ruffle her up five years ago.

Not helpful. Definitely not helpful to think about how I like the way she looks when she's messy. How it makes me think of sex, and how I can remember the way her skin smelled when I kissed her neck while I was buried in her pussy.

"I have never used excel," Chelsea said, clearly annoyed. "I had to watch a bunch of tutorial videos. And the only printer I had access to was in the lobby. And it was out of ink, so I had to run across town to find the right kind, but apparently your printer in the lobby is ancient, so I had to go to a second-hand used tech shop. And then—"

"Great," I said. I slid the stack of papers directly from the corner of my desk and into my trash can. "You can go home now."

Chelsea's eye twitched. "Is that a trash can?"

I looked down at the papers, which were now smeared with some yogurt and rubbing elbows with a banana peel. "Yes."

Chris was biting his fist from the couch, eyes darting between us like I was the opponent in one of Chelsea's old tennis matches. He looked like he didn't know whether to wince or laugh. Distantly, I wondered if this would be the final straw for Chelsea.

Was she going to quit right here? Right now? And why did that idea make me feel a spike of regret?

She turned and walked out of the office without another word.

"Why'd you throw away her papers?" Chris asked.

"Why don't you focus on what you can control. Like this situation with your coach. Has it improved?"

"What, the whole thing where he said he wouldn't re-sign me?"

"Yeah," I said dryly. "That."

"I did think of an idea, but it's probably going to sound stupid."

"Color me shocked."

12

CHELSEA

It was raining, and not the polite kind of rain that makes pretty girls giggle and flip their skirts as they shuffle across the intersection. It was the ugly kind of rain reserved for breakup scenes in romance movies. I'd just watched Damon casually slide hours and hours of my work into his trash can, confirming that he'd only given me the task to screw with me in the first place.

And now it was past midnight. And it was raining.

It meant my grand plans to walk home had been foiled in two ways. The first foil came when my stupidly grumpy and stupidly sexy boss decided to give me a task. Worse, he'd given me a task that clearly wasn't meant to be completed. He had expected me to get frustrated with the enormity and seeming meaninglessness of it. He'd thought I was going to fail, and he'd have his little victory.

And being the eternal dumbass I am, I decided to prove him wrong. Because that's what I always did, wasn't it? Even if it meant having to call my brother and beg him to put Luna to bed for me and promise I'd make it up to him. Even if it meant walking home and taking the subway past midnight in New York City alone because I couldn't afford to waste money on a cab.

Foil number two was the downpour that was hitting the

streets so hard it was coming back up in a frothy white mist. Cars slicked by, blasting little yellow cones of light through the rain and leaving smears of red in the wake of their taillights.

I stood just inside the lobby of the building, waiting for it to magically stop or maybe just calm down enough that I wasn't afraid of being swept into a sewer grate.

"You're still here?" Asked a deep voice from behind me.

Damon was walking out of the building with his hand in his pocket and a jacket slung over his shoulder. Late night or not, he looked as composed and gorgeous as ever. He even smelled delicious, which was impossible to ignore in the tight confines of the little glass box we were standing in beside the doors.

"As long as Mother Nature violently pisses all over the street, yeah."

Damon looked like he was debating something internally, then he sighed. "Come on."

"No."

"I'm not asking."

"And I'm not on the clock. So, no. I'm not going anywhere with you. You're an asshole."

"Yeah, and I try very hard to make sure you and everyone else continues thinking that. But this asshole would rather not have to find a new personal assistant in the morning. If I let you go out there yourself, chances are you'll get mugged or run over by a car."

I sighed. "You're so considerate it hurts."

"Are you going to come with me willingly, or do I need to carry you over my shoulder again?"

I squinted. "Again?"

"Your legs stop working when you get drunk enough, it seems. So what's it going to be, Tinkerbell?"

I crossed my arms but started walking with him. "Why did you take me home when I got drunk, anyway?"

Damon gestured for me to head back inside the building,

toward the stairs leading to the basement parking garage. It made me realize he hadn't happened to pass me on his way out. He'd been heading to the garage when he spotted me over here and came out of his way for me. I wished I wasn't silly enough for that to make butterflies explode in my stomach.

I followed him to the staircase, even though I was deathly afraid of tall staircases. I could always imagine looking up to see a shadowy head pop out from several flights above, followed by hurried footsteps and heavy breathing.

Ugh. My overactive imagination was not my friend at night.

I had to admit I *did* feel safer with Damon around. At least this way, I already knew where the most evil thing in the vicinity was.

We entered into a mostly empty parking garage before he decided to answer. I'd noticed he had a habit of waiting irritatingly long to reply or talk, as if long stretches of silence and the uncomfortable tension it caused were no bother to him.

"I didn't trust Mace with you."

"So, what, you were protecting my virginity?"

He chuckled, as if that was a rich joke. The vague implication that he knew damn well I wasn't a virgin reminded me of exactly how he knew that. Pleasant pulses of heat passed from my chest to my lower stomach. It reminded me how good it had felt to have him take me from behind—and how strong his hands had felt on my hips.

Stop that, Chelsea. Bad, bad girl.

That seemed like another life now. Another Damon. Still an asshole, but he had at least been an asshole who was attracted to me. I guess that wasn't a huge plus on the redemption scale, but it was something.

"Mace has a reputation."

"And you don't?"

He paused outside a dark, expensive looking luxury car. "I learned a few hard lessons about what happens to people who mix business with pleasure. So, no. The only reputation I have now is of being the prick you don't want to get stuck in an elevator with."

"I wasn't going to say anything, but yeah, I can see that. You do smell."

He turned sharply. "What?"

I laughed in surprise to see how vulnerable he looked. "It was a joke. You don't smell. I mean, bad, at least... What cologne do you use anyway?"

Damon composed himself quickly, and he also chose not to reply to my question as he sat down behind the wheel.

I got in the car, smirking a little. "Why is it you want people to hate you, exactly?"

"I never asked anyone to hate me." Damon started the car and began driving. "I don't want to confuse them. I'm their boss. Not a friend. Not a romantic partner. Nothing."

"No wonder you're such a source of joy and happiness."

Damon let out a little grunt of amusement. "I enjoy my work."

"Is that why you stay late so often?"

He paused, as if he was deciding whether he wanted to continue having a candid conversation with me. "I stayed late tonight because my brother is an imbecile. He's one of the top players at the most essential position in the sport with the biggest, most valuable market in the world. He should be like a big ass tree with money growing on it. Instead, it feels like I'm always trying to pull his dumb ass out of trouble."

"Anything I can advise you on? As your personal assistant, of course."

"Your job is to get my coffee and take care of my dry cleaning. Putting out fires is above your paygrade."

"Try me."

Damon sighed. "Chris is too busy partying and chasing women. He has also dipped his interest in the world of drugs recently, which has his coach thinking he'll wind up getting kicked out of the league before long. They're threatening to let him walk after this season. Even if another team picks him up, it'll tank his value. And that's all assuming his coach isn't right—that Chris isn't one failed drug test away from getting kicked out of the league."

I stared ahead as we drove through the torrential rain. Admittedly, I wanted to impress Damon with a good idea. A solution.

"What about some kind of babysitter? No, better than that. Pay someone to pretend to be engaged to him. Make sure she knows she's supposed to keep him away from all the bad stuff. No drugs. No other women. Convince his coaches that he's settling down and he's a new man."

Damon's strong hands flexed on the steering wheel as he sat in silence for an agonizing minute. "That's actually a good idea. It's much better than the plan my brother proposed."

He liked my idea? I made sure I didn't smile like an idiot and clap my hands. Instead, I sat calmly like the kind of person who regularly has great ideas.

"Good. I'm glad I could be helpful. What was your brother's plan?"

Damon surprised me by smiling a little. "He wanted to bribe his coach."

"He really suggested that?"

"My brother has only ever had to focus on football. When it comes to the game, he works his ass off and he's smart as hell. But everything else? I worry about him."

I thought about that. I couldn't quite picture Damon worrying about anything but himself. Then again, I guessed he had left his big fundraiser to personally drive me home. He could've called Dick and asked him to take me home instead, but he'd made sure to do it himself. Maybe I really didn't understand the real Damon.

We reached my brother's place a few minutes later. Damon

surprised me by getting out of his car and walking me to the door.

"Do you want to come in for some coffee or something?" I asked. I wasn't exactly sure why I felt like extending an olive branch, so I figured it was probably self-preservation. If I could manage to stop my relationship with Damon from being a constant sparring match, I could comfortably enjoy the salary. No more fear of getting fired or driven to quit hanging over my head.

Damon arched an eyebrow. "Coffee? It's past midnight."

"Decaf?"

"No. Thank you, but it wouldn't be wise."

Now it was my turn to raise an eyebrow. "What, worried you're going to fall in love with me and violate your sacred code of being a grumpy asshole?"

"Believe what you want, Tinkerbell. I'll see you tomorrow."

For some reason, I found myself smiling and biting my lip when I closed the door. Whatever this was, I needed to stop it. Dangerous didn't even fully capture the stupidity of the spark I felt in my belly.

13

DAMON

I typically managed to avoid my parents, but they eventually pushed hard enough that I had to relent. Unless I wanted to formally cut ties with them, there was no avoiding it.

We were sitting beneath the hanging gardens of a quiet little bistro on the West Side of Manhattan. My father was an aggressively round, red-faced man who had one purpose in life—convince me that I was handling my business wrong. My mother's driving motivation was to get me married and produce an army of grandchildren. Together, they were exhausting.

I checked my phone while we waited for our food. I'd texted Chelsea half an hour ago to ask her to bring me something ridiculous she'd have no hope of accomplishing. I told her to get Tia Klein to meet me here, and with the minuscule time window she had, it was nearly impossible. It was Thursday, and I'd already started to recognize a pattern in my own behavior. When I was pissed or frustrated, I tended to take it out on Chelsea by giving her some sort of impossible assignment. Unfortunately for her, that pretty much meant she was constantly bombarded with tasks.

I felt a little guilty when I saw she still hadn't texted back. I had to admit I was projecting my anger at my parents on her, and she also gave me a legitimately good solution to help with Chris' problem Monday night in the car. But I'd let my guard down too much, so I'd been trying to remind her where we stood ever since then. Maybe I was also trying to remind myself.

Besides, I wasn't going to go soft on her just because she was accidentally useful for once in her life.

"I'm just saying," my father continued between mouthfuls of the crusty bread they'd left on our table. He smeared another generous helping of butter on the piece in his hand, waving his knife as he spoke. "You're trying to sidestep this whole drug and partying thing. I say make it part of his image. Embrace it."

I nodded. In any other context, I'd make my argument to the counter—explain that more than half our sponsors were family brands that'd drop us like we were hot if I tried anything like he was suggesting. But I knew it was easier to play nice and survive these conversations. Fighting back just dragged it out.

My mom pursed her lips a few minutes after my dad trailed off from making his points. "I know that Trish woman made some mistakes, but it really was the last time I saw you happy. Have you ever considered trying to work things out with her?"

I felt my nostrils flare. My parents both knew enough to know how insulting it was to suggest I'd ever try to patch things up with Trish. I knew better, but I couldn't stop myself from speaking my mind.

"No. Trish was the worst thing that ever happened to me. I'd rather die alone and childless than so much as speak to her again."

My mom tutted. "Now you're just being dramatic. You two fought. It's what couples do. You know your father and I fight all the time. Just yesterday he didn't believe me when I said it was going to be cold this winter. But the love bugs came out in force right on schedule, and that always means it's going to be a long, cold winter."

My dad groaned. "You say that every year."

"And what happened two years ago? I was right, wasn't I?"

"You say it every year and you're bound to be right sometimes. What about last year? Hm? Was that a long, cold winter?"

"See?" My mom said, pointing to my dad who was still waiting for an answer. "But we got along well enough to make two wonderful children."

I forced a smile. The rules were different with my parents. I tried to be civil. I tried to play nice. So I shut my mouth and let my mom continue trying to encourage me to go out and impregnate the nearest willing woman.

Shortly after our lunch came, there was a slight commotion among the other people sitting near our table. A group of women got up, rushing to pull out their cameras.

I looked to see what was going on and spotted Chelsea walking arm in arm with Tia Klein.

Holy shit. She actually pulled it off?

Chelsea stopped near our table as Tia finished signing a few autographs and snapping pictures with some of her fans. She gave me a smug wiggle of her eyebrows. "His majesty asks, and he receives."

I couldn't help but laugh. "I'll admit I'm slightly impressed. How did you pull that off?"

"I promised her you'd take her on a date."

My stomach went ice cold. "You... what?"

Chelsea shrugged. "I figured there was no way you'd actually let it happen, so no harm done. But I assumed you wouldn't send such an urgent text if you didn't really, really need her here. Good luck, boss." Chelsea waved over her shoulder and left. She actually walked away, and I was struck by how she might as well be the character in a movie with sunglasses on who walks away from explosions without looking. Because there was sure as hell about to be an explosion.

My parents went as quiet as starstruck children when Tia

came to sit at our table. My mom was probably trying to figure out if Tia was fertile, and my dad was probably wondering if I could sign her to propel my business "to new heights," which was one of his favorite catchphrases. My dad also ran a lawn mowing business, but if you listened to him, he was the Wolf of Wallstreet when it came to business decisions.

Tia was dressed in athletic gear that highlighted her fit body. She was wearing a sports bra that showed off her cleavage and also left her entire, toned midriff bare. "Chelsea tells me you're finally going to take me on that date I've been wanting. I was in the middle of a conditioning session, but for you, I'll make it up later."

I thought about the smug look on Chelsea's face and her blind certainty that I'd turn Tia down. She thought she was setting me up for disaster, and she was proud as hell of herself for it.

I had to weigh my options. I could turn down Tia and risk a fragile new relationship with my best bet at a replacement for my brother if he went off the rails. Or... I could go on the damn date and enjoy every moment of watching Chelsea squirm.

It should've been an easy choice, but for some reason, the idea of potentially sleeping with Tia felt wrong. I kept imagining how Chelsea would feel, which was ridiculous.

I wasn't obligated to protect her. The only legitimate reason to avoid the date would be the obvious conflict with my policy of keeping work and relationships as far apart as possible. The scars Trish left were still fresh enough in my mind to tell me exactly why I should respect that policy.

But this was just a date.

Tia was still waiting, patiently watching me for an answer. I leaned back in my chair and shrugged. "Sure. One date can't hurt."

There. Is that what you really wanted, Chelsea? Because it sure as hell doesn't feel like what I want.

14

CHELSEA

One of the worst things about being a smart woman is having the full mental capacity to realize when you've been an idiot.

I'd watched Tia Klein flirt with Damon and felt an irrational jealous bite in the center of my soul. Again, it was one of those moments where I was smart enough to know I was being stupid. Or so I'd thought.

I assumed my little maneuver of claiming he'd offered to take her on a date would kill a few birds with a single stone. It'd prove to me that Damon didn't exclusively hate me—he hated all beings with boobs and vaginas. It'd also prove to him that he should stop trying to screw with me, because I'd happily screw back.

I'd been walking nervous circles on the tennis court where I was giving a late-night lesson to a grouchy boy who didn't want to be there. I stopped walking, scrunching up my face. No. There would be no screwing back. That was a poor choice of words and a mental image I definitely didn't need right now.

The last problem with my genius little plan was that it was supposed to expel any doubts I had about Damon from my mind.

Even if he did take Tia out and treat her to some of that mind-blowing, pushed up against the wall, sweaty and ferocious sex he'd given me five years ago... Even if that happened, I wouldn't care. And I wouldn't care because I didn't have feelings for him.

Like a well-planned out activity with a toddler, all I could do was watch as everything came down in flames around me.

"Are we done, or what?" Aiden asked from the other side of the court. He was ten years old, out of shape, and a video game enthusiast. His father only signed him up with lessons from me to try to sneak some exercise into his life.

I groaned. As much as I wanted to wallow and keep trying to imagine what Damon and Tia were probably doing right this very moment, I needed to take my job seriously. All of my jobs.

I still hadn't earned my first paycheck from being Damon's personal assistant, and as a single mom, I couldn't afford to take chances with my financial future. That meant continuing to keep up as many of my side gigs as I possibly could. It was Thursday night, and I needed to survive until next Friday until I got paid. Eight days. Seven and some change, if I counted by the hours.

Besides, hitting tennis balls and being on the court was something that always made me feel happy. I barely even felt the small sting of bitterness when I remembered how I'd had to walk away from it all when I still felt like I could accomplish more.

"Can I sit down if we're just going to stand around?" Aiden asked from the other side of the net.

With a sigh, I started whacking balls toward him and watched as he did his best impression of a crippled, elderly woman on her way to a department store she had no coupons for.

This was my life.

As much as I tried, I kept thinking about Damon and Tia. I wondered if they already had their clothes off, or if maybe they weren't to that part of the evening yet.

. . .

For some reason, Richard "Call me Dick" had given me his card. I'd almost forgotten until I got home and found it in my nightstand.

After a brief and ultimately fruitless internal dialogue about minding my own business and why I definitely shouldn't be wondering what my boss' penis is up to tonight, I gave in to temptation. I grabbed my things and begged my brother to come over just in case Luna woke up needing something after I put her to bed. Half an hour later, I found myself riding shotgun with Dick in his ridiculous lifted car.

My conversation with Dick had been brief. Did he know where Damon liked to take his dates?

Hell yes, he did.

Was he willing and able to take me on a ride to said places?

Did a rooster get hard when he walked into the hen house?

I guessed that meant "yes," because Dick had hung up the phone and arrived half an hour later.

"So, how do you know Damon, exactly?" I asked.

Dick was still wearing a name tag that said, "Hi, I'm BIG DICK." I tried to picture him as a young man but couldn't quite manage it.

Dick shrugged at my question. "Damon gave me a job. That's how I know him." He had a wheezy, almost high-pitched voice that didn't completely fit his large, bent over frame.

"So he didn't just hire you to screw with me?"

"Oh, no. I do all kinds of shit for him. I used to beg on the street for spare change. Right outside his building, actually. I guess he got tired of having to carry around coins and figured he'd put me on the payroll to save himself the ass ache. Mr. Rose has been good to me."

I frowned, waiting for Dick to laugh and tell me he'd been joking. "I'm sorry," I said after a few seconds. "It sounded like you said Damon did something nice. I've never seen him show a hint of kindness. Are we talking about the same Damon Rose?"

"Tall, grumpy, stares at you like he wishes he had a toilet to flush you down?"

"Yeah. That sounds like him."

Dick nodded. "Damon's not as bad as he lets on. The poor bastard had his heart ripped out when Trish left Rose Athletic. Took half his clients with her and tried to trash his reputation when she did, too."

I frowned. "What? How did she do that?"

Dick glanced over at me, then shook his head slightly. "Bossman probably wouldn't want me talking about it. Pretend I never mentioned that. All I'm trying to say is he has to be careful. Man in his position... You get a lot of predatory people looking to take advantage. Can't blame the poor bastard for pushing everyone away."

I wished I could pry for more information, but I didn't want to put Dick in an uncomfortable position.

I grinned out the window. If I didn't have the sense of humor of a middle schooler, that thought wouldn't have amused me so much.

Dick pulled up to the curb outside a few of Damon's usual spots. My job was to get out of the car and pathetically stick my head into multiple clubs and restaurants where I scanned the buildings for his obnoxiously handsome face.

The truth was I had no idea what I was actually doing.

What was I going to do if I found them? Charge up to their table or whatever bathroom they were fucking in? Was I going to loudly demand they stop, because I'd been a stubborn idiot for setting them up in the first place? And what argument did I have, anyway? I wasn't even close to admitting to *myself* that I had anything approaching feelings for Damon.

But if that was true, why did I feel like I was losing my mind? Why was I tormenting myself with images of their lips pressed together and his hands roaming her body like I wished they'd roam mine.

I sighed. I may not know what the hell I was doing, but I knew I was going to do something, because I'd lose my mind if I had to sit around and keep wondering.

So in the famous words of many a porn star, I said screw it. I was going in, and I was going in hard.

15

DAMON

Tia Klein was interesting. I may not have had any intent to sleep with her, but from a business standpoint, I was enjoying our conversation. I learned more about her business model and how she leveraged everything she did on her social media. According to her, the plan was to have a solid foundation she could keep taking advantage of long after she'd left the world of sports behind and her beauty had faded.

It seemed like my instincts to pursue her had been spot on. It should've thrilled me, but I still felt vaguely unsettled. She was making no secret of where she expected this to go. She clearly wanted to work together, but she also expected us to fuck around. The question was whether she was willing to allow one of those things to happen without the other.

But that was a bridge I'd cross when I reached it. For now, I was surprised to be enjoying the conversation. She had the right kind of mind for this line of work, and I was beginning to think I was wrong when I thought she couldn't eventually fill the shoes of my brother.

We were sitting in a historical restaurant full of wood paneling, crystal chandeliers, and waiters scurrying around with sizzling plates of steak smothered in butter.

Tia had gone all out with a black, low cut dress and what I had to guess was nearly a hundred grand in jewelry. When she thought I wasn't looking, she'd tug down on her dress to release more of her impressive chest.

And all my dumbass could think about was Tinkerbell.

"Am I boring you, Damon?" Tia managed to combine annoyance and flirtation in the way she balanced her smooth chin on the back of her hand. Her slanted, bright eyes cut into me.

"No. I've got a lot on my mind lately, I apologize. It sounds like you're going to be an amazing fit."

"Oh," she said, her lips spreading. "You have no idea."

I wanted to sigh at my careless choice of words. She still thought this was sexual. Before I had to think of what to say, I heard raised voices in the lobby.

Chelsea was having a heated discussion with one of the waiters, who was now pointing sternly toward the door. She caught my eyes, then a look of determination passed over her face.

Chelsea fast-walked past the waiter and came right up to our table. "Hi, Tia," she said.

I looked Chelsea up and down. She was wearing pajama bottoms and a light blue, mismatched top. If I wasn't mistaken, she wasn't even wearing a bra, and she definitely hadn't brushed her hair. I saw now why the waiter was trying to keep her out.

"Hey, girl. Everything okay?" Tia asked.

"No, actually." Chelsea shifted her weight, then ran her tongue over her teeth. She opened her mouth to speak, then bit her lip and sighed. "Mr. Rose, there's an emergency at the office. A big one."

"An emergency at the office?" I asked.

"A big one," she repeated with a nod.

I slid my eyes to Tia, who was watching with an unreadable expression. I had no idea what kind of emergency there could be at the office, considering I was the last one to leave. Unless one of the janitors slipped and fell, she had to be bullshitting me.

"I should really go check on this," I said.

Tia set her napkin down. "In the middle of our date?"

"As your agent, you should consider it a plus that I don't let anything come before the business."

She pursed her lips, and for some reason, I thought she had taken what I just said as a challenge.

I fished some money out of my pocket and set it down on the table. "We'll catch up soon, Tia."

Tia smiled, and I was relieved to see she didn't appear angry. Instead, there was a calculating look behind her eyes. That was a problem I'd need to unpack later, I decided. For now, I had to figure out whatever was urgent enough to drag Chelsea out of bed and get her to hunt me down.

Chelsea, who had been silent during our exchange, followed me out to the street. The angry waiters who seemed to be forming a plan to remove her relented when they saw I was walking her out.

Outside, I rounded on her. "Do you realize how fragile my relationship with Tia is still? What if she cuts ties with Rose and goes to another agency now?"

Chelsea folded her arms, which had the unfortunate effect of drawing my eyes to her breasts. Yeah. Definitely no bra, and definitely fantastic.

No. Stop looking. Stop thinking about how a good, quick fuck would probably do wonders for the both of you.

"Well?" I asked.

Chelsea shrugged in a way that was admittedly adorable. "Sorry, okay? I can be a little impulsive sometimes."

"That's it? You... Wait, how did you even know where to find me? And why does it look like you rolled out of bed to come here. And how would you even know if there was an emergency at work if you came from home?"

"These are all good questions," Chelsea said with a slow, diplomatic edge to her voice. "One could argue that another good question is why you went on a date with that woman?"

I felt like I was about to lose my mind in a violent explosion of expletives. "Seriously? You're being completely serious right now? You are the one who cornered me into going on the goddamn date in the first place!" I realized I was shouting, which had drawn the looks of a few people passing on the street. Given that it was New York, nobody was interested enough in our drama to stop and listen.

"I screwed up. Okay? I don't know what was going through my head, but I shouldn't have done that. And, yeah… I might have made up the thing about the emergency. And yes, I might've come from my bed. And I might've had to grill Dick to find out where you were."

"You grilled… dick? What the fuck are you even talking about? Is that some kind of sick innuendo? Did you sleep with someone?"

Chelsea, who had looked like she was on the verge of tears, burst out laughing. "Grilling dick? Do you think that's what the kids say these days? No. I mean I had to ask your formerly homeless friend, Richard. He also gave me a ride."

I relaxed. Thinking about her sleeping with someone else, no matter how stupid I'd been to jump to the conclusion, had made me want to break something. What the hell was this woman doing to me?

"You're an obstinate pain in my ass, and I should fire you."

Chelsea lifted her chin but didn't say anything to defend herself.

I felt some of the anger drain out of me. "And it was resourceful. Finding me like you did. Also, the way you pitted Tia against me with the date thing. You've got an edge to you that impresses me as much as it pisses me off."

She narrowed her eyes. "Is this the 'you're fired' speech?"

"No. But you did make me leave the restaurant before I got to eat. Now I'm starving. So unless you want it to turn into the 'you're fired' speech, I suggest you contact Dick and get him to take us somewhere I can get a meal."

She smiled, almost cautiously. "You want to eat a meal with me? Are you going to poison my food when I'm not looking?"

"I never said I want to eat it with you. But I will allow you to eat at the same time as me. I also haven't decided about the poison yet."

She clapped her hands and gave me a quick hug. I stood there like an idiot while she pressed her small body to mine, squeezing.

I officially didn't understand the woman. It wasn't the first time she'd flipped from looking like she was about to punch me in the face to hugging me, and I had no idea how I was supposed to read it.

Chelsea was a closed book. She was a closed book I happened to have fucked five years ago, but other than that, I had a feeling I didn't know the first thing about her.

Why did that still bother me so much?

16

CHELSEA

Damon sat across from me at an all-night breakfast place. The dominant color scheme seemed to be mustard yellow with a side of depression. I was sure Damon was in his own special hell, especially since his not-so-favorite color was everywhere. But I was starving, and the pile of pancakes in front of me looked like the most delicious thing on Earth. Well, assuming I wasn't allowed to enter Damon into the contest.

Yes. I was gradually coming to terms with the fact that I was violently, ferociously, unreasonably attracted to the man. I was drawn to him like a fly to the neon blue light. Except I couldn't even plead ignorance like a fly could.

I knew what was going to happen if I ever managed to get closer to him. I'd float in, eyes wide and brain blasting me with warnings about bad ideas and stupid decisions. Each flap of my stupid little wings would bring me closer, until…

Zap.

That's what he was. He was a trap in a designer suit. A devil with the face of an angel. Oh, and he was the father of my child.

I dug into my pancakes, drizzled another obscene helping of syrup on top of the stack, and chewed. I decided the whole fatherhood thing could be my excuse. I mean, didn't I have some sort of maternal duty to really give the guy a chance to prove he was more than Lucifer made flesh?

Damon scowled at his waffles.

"You eat them," I explained, pantomiming what he should do with his knife and fork.

"I ordered chocolate chip waffles."

I grinned. "Yeah, I know. You child."

He glared up at me. "These are blueberry."

"Want to trade or something? I'll eat them."

Damon looked at my plate with disgust. In his defense, I had a stack of about eight pancakes in front of me that were swimming in a shallow pool of syrup. I'd also indiscriminately slathered globs of butter here and there.

"No? Then I guess you'll just have to deal with it."

He sighed, grabbed his plate, and walked up to the counter.

I waited for the tongue lashing I knew was about to come. I nearly pressed my fingers in my ears and squeezed my eyes shut, but both actions would've reduced the speed I could inhale my pancakes, so I didn't.

I chewed, eyes wide as I watched the impending explosion.

Damon got a young teenage guy's attention behind the counter. He was too far for me to actually hear what he was saying, but I was surprised when he didn't start by throwing fists. Instead, he seemed to be talking in a normal voice as he pointed to his plate.

The kid nodded, smiled, and took the plate.

When Damon sat back down, I waited.

"What?" he demanded.

"Were you being polite?"

"I had to wait tables before all this. You can be the biggest ass on the planet and get a pass from me, but people who are rude to customer service workers deserve a special place in hell."

I grinned. "Wait, so first I find out you hired a homeless man to help him. Now I learn you're some sort of saint patron of the customer service industry?"

"I tried to tell you. The way I am serves a purpose at work."

"And what about the fact that you seem to have no interest in women? Does that serve a purpose?"

He paused. "No interest in women?"

I shrugged. "It's just something I've noticed. And there's a little workplace gossip, too. People say you haven't really dated or anything in years."

"People should mind their own business."

"So what is it?" I knew Damon was trying to get me to stop prying, but I also knew I was going to drive myself crazy if I didn't get answers soon. "Someone broke your heart and now you are locking it away as a precaution?"

He just stared at me, his sharp jaw ticking as he clenched his teeth and relaxed them. Clench. Relax. Clench.

"Is that it?" I asked. I felt angry. He'd slept with me five years ago. Maybe it didn't mean anything to him, but it had been damn near impossible for me to forget. He'd given me a daughter, and even if he didn't know it, the man was a bastard for being so cold and callous. "You're too scared to get hurt again? Well guess what, people's feelings get hurt. That's life. You won't ever know if someone is right for you if you never put your heart on the line. You've got to risk it to make it happy."

Damon's calm finally evaporated. "You don't know the first thing about me. And don't pretend to lecture me on the finer points of love when you've clearly only experienced the failing side of it."

My stomach went icy. "Excuse me?"

"You have a daughter. The father is gone. Who are you exactly to lecture me on the merits of relationships?"

I briefly considered flipping my plate in his face. Maybe it would've been more satisfying to frisbee a half-eaten, sticky pancake at his forehead. Both options would mean wasting my food, so I angrily pulled out a thick stack of napkins from the dispenser. I lifted my pancakes with my bare hands, set them on the napkins, and stood. I almost walked out without saying anything, but I stopped long enough to wave my pancakes at him and glare. "You know? You think this asshole thing is an act or something you use to run your business better. But I think you've been pretending so long that it became real." I took two steps toward the door, then walked back to the table. "And what kind of grown ass man orders chocolate chip waffles? You're a child, Damon. A child in a confusingly big package, but a child."

I walked out while reflecting on how I probably didn't need to say that last part.

I didn't care though. I hated the man.

It wasn't his rudeness that made me hate him, either. I hated him because he'd put a baby in me five years ago, and now I knew I was going to go through hell and everything in between to find out who he really was. I hated him because I had to keep trying. I especially hated him because my body had decided to go rogue when Damon Rose was involved.

I could want to punch him in his stupidly perfect nose one minute and wish he'd bend me over the nearest table and take me from behind the next.

Damon Rose could go screw himself for all I cared. I'd only be a little tempted to watch him try.

17

DAMON

I stared out the window of the conference room. Manhattan sprawled out as far as I could see, cutting clear, geometric shapes against blue skies.

And there was a young guy in his mid-twenties washing the window on a scaffold attached to pulleys. Most of my senior administration staff was sitting around the long conference table and debating about how we should handle a contract dispute between one of our athletes and their biggest sponsor.

I was uncharacteristically distracted, though, because the window washer was making a heart shaped pattern every time he wiped his cleaning fluid off the window. When I followed his stupid gaze and equally stupid grin, it appeared to be aimed at none other than fucking Tinkerbell, who was sitting to my right and facing the window.

I tapped her leg under the table and shot her a look.

She frowned down at the table, then up at me. "Footsie? Really, Damon?" she whispered. "You're lucky I wore clean socks today." She added with a wiggle of her eyebrows.

"Try paying attention, Tinkerbell."

"You first."

I sat back in my chair. Why did her attitude always seem to stir up the wrong emotions in me? I should've wanted to fire her on the spot, but instead I found myself wondering which hand I'd fist her hair with while she bobbed her head up and down on my cock.

Pathetic. Apparently, this was what staying celibate for too long caused. I could barely keep it in my pants around her, and I had no idea what about her drove me so wild.

I found myself studying her, from the pixie-like features to the curvy shape I could remember having to myself five years ago. I thought about the way she'd felt so damn tight and warm around me, and how good it had felt to hear the way she hadn't been able to stop the moans from slipping free when she came on my cock.

Chelsea raised an eyebrow. I realized then she was watching me watch her. "Are you that jealous of the window washer? Should I go see if he'll give me a kiss to go with those hearts?"

I looked at the window washer, who was craning his neck to see if Chelsea was paying attention to his antics. I got up suddenly, then yanked the blinds closed. Everyone else looked up at me.

"The sun was in my eyes." I grumbled, sitting down.

"Those windows face the West, Mr. Rose," Chelsea said in an obnoxiously flat tone. "It's ten in the morning."

I noticed everyone trying very hard to look anywhere but my direction.

"If I need your input, I'll ask for it, Miss Cross. Please focus on taking notes. And do your best to write more legibly. Those notes look like you scribbled them while sitting on one of those vibrating hotel beds."

Chelsea bit back a grin. "Do you have a lot of experience with vibrating hotel beds, Mr. Rose?" She leaned closer, lowering her voice. "Or is it that you can't help imagining me on one of them?"

Was she serious? Apparently, my dick thought so, because it immediately stiffened.

"Keep figuring out our fucking problem," I commanded the rest of the room. I started scribbling something on my notepad, just to avoid having to look at Chelsea for a moment.

When I hired her, I'd intended to drive her out of the office with the slow torture of my proximity. Instead, it felt like she was the one with the upper hand, and I needed to find a way to fix that, and soon. Really damn soon.

I looked down at what I'd written, then grinned with mirth.

Don't be stupid was scratched into the legal pad about ten times.

18

CHELSEA

"Mommy, how long do I have to stay under your desk?"

"Shh!" I grinned stupidly. I was still positioned directly in the center of the office. I had no cubicle walls and no form of privacy. I also had a daughter with a school holiday and no brother to watch her while I worked today.

Maybe the slightly more reasonable thing to do would've been to ask my bosshole for the day off. Instead, I'd come in early enough that I knew only maintenance staff might see that I was accompanied by an adorable little package of curly cuddles.

It also gave me time to position my bag and whatever else I could find to sort of block off the bottom of my desk. Luna was currently down there with my phone to watch and a pair of headphones. We were going on three hours, which was like three years in little kid time.

The office was buzzing with activity by now. Smartly dressed men and women zipped around the room like there were literal fires to put out on their keyboards.

And me? I was muttering answers to a little girl hiding under my desk.

"Do *not* move, okay?" I said.

Luna froze where she was, which caused her small frame to tip over sideways while she acted like she'd just been blasted with ice.

I grinned, then got up. It was Friday, and I'd promised myself I was going to confront Daria before the end of the week. Maybe I saved it for the absolute last minute, but I was a woman of my word, either way.

I found her at her desk in the corner of the room, which was partitioned off like everyone else's, *except mine*. She turned in her chair to regard me when I walked up. I noticed her desk and partition walls were decorated with little skeletons, voodoo heads I hoped were fake, and posters for bands I didn't recognize.

"Oh, it's you," she said dryly.

"Yeah, it's me. The one you told to wear yellow to impress Damon."

Daria's normally flat face changed so slowly I almost didn't realize it was happening. Her full lips were pulled up at one corner in the faintest smile. "And you bit hard on that one, didn't you?"

I sucked in air through my nose, not even sure what to say. "Why? That's all I want to know. *Why?*"

Daria considered me. "You're right. That was mean of me. To tell you the truth, his favorite color is actually plaid. If you *really* want him to be nice, wear that tomorrow."

I found myself grinning, and Daria grinned back. "Asshole," I muttered, turning to leave.

"Gullible," she called after me.

I got back to my desk, still not sure if I was mad at Daria or starting to like her. I tapped Luna, who was still frozen in place. "Unfreeze," I whispered.

She blew out a breath of relief, then went back to watching her phone.

That was when Damon's incomprehensible email came in.

. . .

Tink, (not only did he still use a little pet name for me, we'd apparently moved on to a pet name within the pet name? Things were getting serious, clearly.)

I have a client coming in today and she's lactose intolerant, glucose sensitive, and only eats food with an "identifiable history." I want an impressive assortment of things for her to snack on while she's here. You have an hour.

Damon

I stared at my screen, ignoring the fact that Luna was literally gnawing on my ankle. Sometimes I swore she was part dog, part child.

What the hell did it mean for food to have an identifiable history? Secondly, how was I going to manage to not only find that sort of thing but do it within an hour? More importantly, I also needed to do this impossible task without alerting anyone that I'd snuck my daughter into work today.

I ducked my head down below my desk so I could see Luna. She popped an earbud out and stopped gnawing on my leg long enough to look up. "Yes, Mommy?"

"If I ask one of my worker friends to watch you for a little while, can you promise to be good?"

"I'll only be good for that one."

Luna pointed past the box I'd set near my bag to block her off from view. I followed her little finger and saw she was pointing to a beautiful blonde woman I'd never met. I groaned.

"I don't know that lady. I can't trust someone I don't know to watch you."

"You said this place was safe."

Damn it. Kids had a way of weaponizing your own words. Luna was a weapons expert, too. "It is safe, but it would make mommy feel better if it was someone I know keeping an eye on you."

"Fine. I want him."

This time, I turned around to find about six feet and four inches of bosshole standing behind me. Glorious smelling, dripping with sexuality, and fuming bosshole.

"Oh, hi," I said.

"Hi," Luna echoed.

I was dead. I was about to be thrown through the paneled windows to crash on the streets. If I was lucky, maybe I could pull one of those stunts from movies where I bounce off a few conveniently placed fabric overhangs.

Probably not. With my luck, I'd more likely end up falling through a sewer grate and getting hit by a train. I wondered which was technically faster. The ground racing up to meet you or a speeding subway train.

"Hello?" Damon asked. "Do you care to explain this?"

Luna angled her phone toward him. "That's Gibblet. He gets into all kinds of trouble because he is always breaking things. See?" She let out an adorable little chuckle as the hairy creature in her show started to disassemble the car of a pig who was waiting for a red light. "He wants to know how it works," she added, still laughing.

To my surprise, Damon was smirking. "I took apart my dad's watch once. My brother told me there were little people in there who kept track of the time, and I wanted to see them."

"What were they like?" Luna asked.

I smiled, forgetting everything except that my daughter was looking at her father and he was smiling back at her. Of course, neither of them knew it. They were just talking, and my heart hurt because it felt so painfully right.

"They were super small and very cute. You should take apart one of your mommy's watches when she isn't looking to meet them for yourself."

Damon straightened, then focused back on me. "Do you have the food yet?"

Was he not going to mention Luna? He wasn't even going to ask about it?

"Um, not quite yet. I just needed to—"

"You need someone to keep an eye on her while you go get it? We'll figure it out. But you need to go now if you want to be back in time."

"You're sure?"

"Go, Tinkerbell."

"I love Tinkerbell!" Luna squealed. "Have you seen the one where she makes the whole fairy village tree grow huge?"

"I haven't," Damon said. "Is that one good?"

Luna laughed like he'd just asked the dumbest question imaginable. "If you like fairies."

"Sounds like I'd really enjoy it." Damon's focus shifted to me for a split second, and my stupid brain decided to take that as some sort of secret message.

I was Tinkerbell to him, and he said he'd really enjoy a movie about fairies? Okay, yeah. I was overthinking it. "You're really sure it's okay? And you'll make sure she's okay?"

"Go, Chelsea. And yeah, this is a multi-million-dollar company. Somehow, I think we'll manage to handle keeping a little kid alive for a few hours."

"I'm not little. I can see over the kitchen counter," Luna said crossly.

"Impressive," Damon said. "But how high is the counter in your house? Two feet?"

"I bet I could see over *your* counter."

"You absolutely couldn't. My counter is this high. You won't be able to see over it for years." He held his hand up way above her head.

I watched the two of them argue in a mild state of shock. Even though they were bickering now, it was hilarious. Damon, a full-grown man, was debating whether my daughter was a grown up. He also appeared to be taking the argument completely seriously, just like Luna was.

With a quick prayer that I really could trust a building full of adults to keep Luna alive, I rushed out the door to start on my hopeless task of finding the things Damon asked for.

I had nothing to be smiling about, but I found myself beaming from ear to ear as I half ran out of the building.

19

DAMON

I waited with my fingers threaded together in an inverted "V." Across my desk, a very small, very angry person was testing my patience.

"I won't break it."

"You will."

Luna crossed her arms and stuck her lip out in a pathetic attempt to draw sympathy from me. Ridiculous. Sure, she looked cute, but so did bunnies on the side of the road. I wasn't about to let a bunny handle the handmade glass paperweight one of my clients had given me as a gift a few years back. It was an intricately carved sculpture of an athlete winding up to throw a baseball, and I happened to enjoy looking at it.

"You might as well give up. You won't win this," I said.

"I held a snow globe once," Luna said.

"And?"

"Snow globes are glass. I didn't break it."

"If you had petted a tiger once without getting bit, it doesn't mean I'd be enthused about letting you try again."

"You've petted a tiger?" Luna's eyes lit up, and it was clear she'd completely moved on from the idea of holding my paperweight.

I decided to seize the opportunity and divert her, just to avoid circling back to her touching my things. It seemed that negotiating with small people was very similar to bargaining with high power athletes, multi-million-dollar teams, and huge corporations.

It also happened that I was damn good at it.

"I didn't just pet a tiger. I held a baby one and fed it milk from a bottle."

I thought Luna's already large eyes couldn't get any wider, but she proved me wrong. "A baby tiger?" she whispered.

My mouth twitched. Maybe it was a smile, but it probably wasn't. "That's right."

"You can come to my birthday party if you let me touch him."

"The tiger? This was years ago."

"I want to touch him. Please Mr. Flower."

"Rose. And you're not understanding me."

"Tiger. I want to touch one."

I sighed. For the briefest moment, I felt sympathy for Chelsea. She had to deal with this force of nature at home and then come to work to put up with me? Maybe I could go a little easier on her from now on. Just slightly, though.

"We'll see," I said, fully intending that to actually mean "it's never going to happen."

But Luna jumped up from her chair and punched at the sky. "Yes! Thank you!" She started trying to climb up and over my desk, so I had to get out of my chair and go help her down. As soon as I was beside her, she gave up and spun to hug my legs.

I shook my head at the ceiling. Apparently, spontaneous happiness and hugs were genetic qualities Chelsea passed on to her disturbingly cute spawn.

Not for the first time, I wondered what kind of man her father was. I also wondered if he knew what kind of daughter he had.

For some reason, the thought made me sad, so I decided to focus on something else.

"Where's your mom?" I asked, peeling Luna off my leg.

She dropped into a fighting stance and started swatting at my hands, as if I'd just challenged her to a duel. "Hi-Cha!" she squealed, aiming a kick at my knee.

I put my hand on her forehead, keeping her out of range while she flailed uselessly. "Are you done yet?"

Luna nodded, so I removed my hand. That was exactly when she dashed into range and karate chopped my leg.

Normally, I hate kids. In fact, I was pretty sure if this particular gremlin gave me enough time, I'd find a way to hate her too. But for some inexplicable reason, I found myself pretending her attack had mortally wounded me. I gripped my knee, let out a silent scream, and fell to the floor of my office.

Luna squealed with glee and jumped on my stomach. She started a deadly combo of punches and head butts. I played it up, grunting and twitching with each hit.

And that was exactly when Chelsea walked into my office with bags and bags of assorted food hanging from her straining arms.

I set Luna to the side and stood as quickly and with as much dignity as I possibly could. I cleared my throat. "You found everything I asked for?"

Chelsea said nothing, but her eyes went between Luna and I several times while her mouth split into a crooked grin. "You two were playing?"

"Mr. Daisy is fun," Luna said with a happy little nod.

"Rose," I growled.

Chelsea hesitated, then dropped all her things on the side table. "I couldn't really find food that was... whatever she was talking about. But it's all organic."

"It's fine," I said. "Can you take this thing home?"

Luna laughed. "I'm not a thing. I'm a girl. Mommy, I like him. He's silly. And he has a tiger!"

"Take this girl back home, then. You can have the rest of the day off."

"Wait, what?" Chelsea asked. "Aren't you going to root through the stuff I brought and tell me what a donkey I am for getting it wrong? I already wrote a little speech to use for when you start insulting me. I was going to lead with the fact that this vein on the side of your forehead bulges when you get mad, and how—"

"Chelsea. Go home. Take Luna. And this looks great. Good enough, I mean."

She tilted her head. "Then I'm going to tentatively say thank you. But I can retract it if this turns out to be one of your tricks."

"Fair. Now please leave."

Chelsea crossed the room like she was going to hug me again. I put my hand out, catching her in the chest before she could reach me. "No hugging necessary. I'm your boss, not your friend, remember?"

Chelsea's cheeks went red. "Right, sorry. No hugs for bosses. Even when they are nice for a change. I promise I won't try it again."

I nodded, then pulled my hand back.

With surprising quickness, Chelsea slipped toward me and squeezed me in a hug. "Sorry. Couldn't help it." It might've irritated me, but I was amused at how similar the move was to the one Luna had just pulled when she karate chopped my legs minutes earlier.

"Hugs!" Luna squealed. "I love 'em!" I felt tiny arms wrap around my thigh.

I wasn't smiling. Maybe I was having some sort of stroke or just baring my teeth. But I definitely wasn't smiling.

20

CHELSEA

"A business trip? With you? For the entire weekend?"

Damon nodded. He was leaning casually against my desk. He'd stripped off his jacket and had the sleeves of his crisp white shirt rolled up below the elbows.

Unfortunately, I was very aware of how tanned, muscular, and strong his arms looked. I swore, men's forearms were like cleavage, except no guy ever got slut shamed for whipping out those meat sticks in public. *No.* Forget the fact that forearms like Damon's could've served as industrial grade lubricant for a room full of women—they didn't have nipples, so it was okay to flaunt them.

"Are you alright?" Damon asked. "You look pale. More than usual."

I glared. *I'd be okay if you put those things away. And if I could stop remembering how it felt to have your big ass, strong hands gripping my waist while you bent me over.*

Why was it I couldn't remember one of the two items I went into the grocery store for, but I could vividly remember every minute detail about sleeping with Damon *five years* ago? It still felt like another life. If Luna wasn't walking proof that it had happened, I might not even believe it anymore.

"I'm perfectly fine. But why me?" I asked.

"You're my personal assistant. I may need assistance in Savannah."

I opened my mouth to protest but couldn't think of a valid argument. "What about Luna? I still haven't even got my first paycheck, and I can't ask my brother to watch her for that long."

"I'll cover the expense. You can pick any nanny you want. Or we can pay your brother for his time. But I need you on this trip."

I'd been half turned in my chair, but I fully gave him my attention then. "You *need* me?"

"Professionally speaking. Yes." Damon's dark hair was neatly cut and pushed away from his forehead. As always, he looked like the picture of a man in his prime. He practically radiated health and sexuality, and I felt equal parts drawn to going anywhere he asked and compelled to run as fast as I could.

"Call me crazy," I said. "But it feels like the only things you've asked me to do since I started here are meant to annoy me. So do you actually need me, or do you need an outlet for your endless supply of spite?"

"I don't have time to babysit your ego. If you want to keep your job, you'll be ready to board a plane with me at noon tomorrow. Just give me the name of whoever you need to watch Luna and I'll make sure they're compensated."

Damon left me at my desk to glower at nothing in particular. What a dickbag.

I still didn't buy it, though. Some degree of his personality was an act, and I was determined to prove it. I felt like I needed to know more about this woman who supposedly turned him so cold.

As far as I could tell, he'd sworn off sex, relationships, and compassion. What makes a guy do something like that?

Once I was sure he was back in his office—he was, because I

could hear his deep voice through the door as he berated someone over the phone—I pulled up my internet browser.

I typed "Damon Rose breakup" into the search bar. Before I even finished typing the query, it auto filled with "Damon Rose breakup Trish Jameson."

Trish Jameson... I copy pasted her name into a new tab and pulled up an image search.

Beautiful. Of course she was beautiful. She had dark hair and looked flawless, even in candid paparazzi shots. She had an upturned nose, high cheekbones, full lips, and boobs that didn't appear to have been introduced to gravity yet. I wanted to roll my eyes.

Very typical, Damon. Did you pick this one out of a magazine?

I switched over to looking the woman herself up. Apparently, she'd been one of the first agents he hired on. The article I was reading had an earlier picture of her, probably from around the time she started working for him. She looked beautiful before what must've been her recent hobby of plastic surgery visits. I decided to give Damon a little more of a pass for his taste.

She'd started working for Damon only a few months after he and I met five years ago. They dated, things got pretty serious, and then in some kind of blowup, she managed to leave Rose Athletic with most of his biggest clients. Surprisingly, it was just like Dick had said, but no matter how much I searched, I couldn't seem to find out why they'd broken up or how she managed to walk away with his clients.

I leaned back in my chair and threaded my fingers behind my head.

Hmm. What happened, Damon? Whatever it was, I decided a weekend trip was probably going to be my best shot to dig the information out of him, one way or another.

. . .

I MADE AN IRRITATED SOUND AND PRESSED ON MY EARS, WISHING THE clogged feeling would pass. We'd just reached cruising altitude, and I had already played through about a thousand ways this airplane could end my existence. My favorite scenario was a castaway situation where Damon and I had to gradually strip off our clothes to create ropes and whatever else we needed. By day two, he'd be wearing shreds of fabric that barely concealed piles of rippling, angry muscles. Every time he looked at my sun-bronzed skin, he'd pop an aggressive erection that would burst through his torn pants.

By day three, he'd be overcome with lust at the sight of my aggressively average physique and he'd take me by the sand dunes.

And then I'd shake myself, because Damon was a bad idea. Sex with Damon, even casually, was a bad idea. The man seemed to have some sort of superhuman fertility powers, and chances were, if he got that baby stick near me again, I'd wind up with another muffin in the oven.

No, thank you, Lucifer. One baby without a father was enough.

"Would you stop fidgeting?" Damon snapped. He pressed his hand on my knee, which continued to shake up and down.

I decided to ignore the pleasant feeling his hand on my knee stirred up. *Nope. Not happening, Chelsea.*

"Do you think planes can fly with one engine?" I asked.

"What, are you afraid of flying?"

"No. I'm afraid of falling."

He set down his phone and whatever he'd been looking at on it. "That's stupid."

I glared at him. "If you're trying to be comforting, you're failing at it about as much as I'd expect."

"What I mean is you're more likely to die from a car crash on the highway than up here."

"Yeah, but at least I'd be behind the wheel. On a plane, I'm helpless. What if a murder of geese decides to take us out? Revenge for the car park that replaced their favorite lake?"

"A murder of geese? Are you serious? That's crows."

"Crows wouldn't be this high."

"Neither would geese!" Damon raised his voice, then took a breath and seemed to calm himself. "The term is a murder of crows. Geese would be a flock. And neither would be at this altitude. The air is too thin."

I pondered this. "An asteroid then. One rogue asteroid and that's it. We're toast."

"Do I need to give you busy work to take your mind off this?"

"Can I watch a movie on your phone?"

"Can you—" He stopped mid-sentence, blinked slowly, as if gathering strength, then shook his head. "No. You cannot touch my phone. Use your own."

"Mine's low on charge and I don't want to use the last of it incase Grant needs to call me about Luna. Why can't I use yours, anyway? Do you have nudes on your camera roll you don't want me to see? Did you forget I've already seen everything? *Everything*," I added in a sinister whisper.

Damon glanced to the side, as if to see if the other fancy business people flying first class were listening in. "I've seen everything you have to offer, too, Tinkerbell. And as your boss, I'd advise you to do what I did. Try to purge it from your memory banks."

I knew I shouldn't tease him, but I couldn't stop myself. "No, thanks. I like those images right where they are."

Damon did a double take, then looked back at his phone. A few seconds later, I glanced down at his lap and noticed a distinct bulge pressing against his pants.

His mouth could lie, but his cock couldn't. He still wanted it. The real question was whether I did—aside from silly beachside fantasies.

. . .

We touched down in the city of Savannah in the late afternoon. It was pleasant, sunny, and a little breezy. If I ignored the icy chill radiating from Damon, it was almost perfect.

We were driven to a hotel downtown, let in by friendly staff at the doors, and pointed toward the elevators. When we reached our floor, Damon handed me a key.

"Room 317. That's my lucky number," I said, twirling the keycard and it's lanyard on my finger.

"No. 317 is my room. You're supposed to be in 318."

I double checked the card. "Says 318."

Damon frowned down at his. With a low growling noise, he pushed past me and headed for the elevators. I decided to let myself in the room while he sorted things out.

It was clearly the room he intended for himself, because it was massive. There was a gigantic bed, a sitting area, a little writing desk with a cute antique lamp, and gorgeous views of the city below.

I hopped on the bed and turned on the TV. Coming for this weekend trip meant I'd had to cancel a handful of tennis lessons and my bartending shift on Sunday. But when I complained to Damon about it, he scribbled me a check for two thousand dollars. Then he actually asked if that was enough to cover my time.

Of course, I'd nodded and waited until he wasn't watching to do the Carlton dance by my desk. I didn't even know how to do the Carlton, so I basically just spasmed and fidgeted with joy for a full minute. I'd also rushed to the bank immediately after work and cashed that bad boy. I bought Luna a toy on the way home, picked up a nice takeout dinner for my brother, and paid two bills I was late on. I also electronically paid Milly back the seven dollars I'd owed her for two years and lived in eternal dread of her remembering. She'd bought me a burrito at the mall once when I forgot my money.

All in all, life wasn't so bad. I was even starting to believe I was really going to get my first paycheck when Friday rolled around. Six days. Six days until everything would really start to be okay. It'd be a life changer, and it might mean I could actually drop all the side gigs that were eating up the little time I did have with Luna.

Damon came storming into the room several minutes later. He closed the door behind him, then stared at me. I was sprawled out on the bed and wearing one of the complimentary robes over my clothes. "Comfortable?" he asked.

"Yes, actually. Do I have to go to my room now?"

"No. There was a mistake and they only booked one room."

"There wasn't another one?"

"There's some event going on this weekend. Every hotel in the city is fully booked up. Waiting list only."

I couldn't help grinning. "So you're stuck with me in your room?"

"And you're stuck with me. The bed is mine."

I sighed and started to get up.

"That was a joke. I'll sleep on the couch."

"Oh." I waited, watching him carefully.

Damon was rooting through his suitcase for something. "What?"

"I'm waiting for the catch. You can sleep on the bed, *but*..."

"There's no catch. I'm not going to make you sleep on the couch."

"But you've been going out of your way to make me miserable ever since I started here. Isn't that exactly the kind of thing you'd normally do?"

He set his suitcase down and stood with a few pieces of clothes in his hand. "Yes. Maybe. But I'm going to give being civil to you a try this weekend. As much as I hate to admit it, you have actually handled your responsibilities well. Especially considering my behavior."

"Are you feeling okay?"

"No. Airplanes are disgusting, and I need a shower. So if you'll excuse me."

The bathroom door clicked shut behind him and I heard the water start running.

And in that moment, my castaway fantasy was suddenly and violently shoved aside by a new one. In this one, Damon would emerge from the shower in nothing but a tightly wrapped white towel. The outline of his bulge would be clearly visible just below his sixteen-pack abs. He'd point to something he needed, and the towel would fall, revealing his waiting and ready manhood—which of course would be rock hard from the idea of plowing me into next Tuesday. Actually, I'd prefer if he plowed me straight into Friday so I could pick up my paycheck.

Cha-ching.

I closed my eyes and flopped back onto the bed.

Bad.

Bad, Chelsea.

Or was it bad?

One could make a compelling argument that it'd actually be my motherly duty to sleep with Damon again. And again. And again. *And again.*

After all, he was the father of my daughter. Sure, he was rough around the edges, but who said I couldn't work a little Chelsea magic on him and turn him to the light side? I'd even been told once that my personality was the human equivalent of sandpaper. If I was sandpaper and Damon was rough cut lumber, maybe all we needed was to rub ourselves together until we smoothed each other out.

When Damon emerged from the shower, he was depressingly clothed in a black shirt and running shorts. He even had his tennis shoes all laced up.

"Did you take a shower so you could exercise? Wouldn't it have made more sense to do things the other way around?"

"No. What if sweat carried whatever grime was on me from the airplane into my mouth or eyes?"

I smirked. "Then you'd let your body do what bodies do and deal with it? Are you really a germaphobe? How did I not know this by now?"

"I'm not. It's just airplanes. They're disgusting."

"Right. Well, if you're going for a jog, let me come." I hopped off the bed and went to my suitcase.

Damon eyed me. "No. I was going to go by myself."

"Right. Until I said, 'let me come with you.' What's wrong? Worried you won't be able to keep up?"

He shrugged. "Suit yourself. But I'm not going to slow down for you."

"You won't have to."

21

DAMON

Breathe in through my nose, out through my mouth. I'd learned a long time ago that running was all about letting momentum and gravity do the work for you. Lean forward, lift one knee at a time, extend the foot.

So long as I kept my heart rate down, I could go like this for miles. We'd made it about half a mile when Chelsea's ragged breathing started to become apparent.

She bobbed along beside me with her hair in a tight ponytail. She was wearing a pair of leggings and an athletic top that I found distracting, but I wasn't letting myself dwell on it.

"You doing okay?" I asked.

"Better than you," Chelsea replied between panting breaths.

"Try breathing through your nose."

"My nose?" She sounded incredulous. "It's too small to… give me… the air I need."

I grinned. "You remember how to get back to the hotel, right?"

Instead of speaking, she made a grunting noise of acknowledgment.

"See you there." I ran on, noticing how quickly she was falling behind now. For the next mile or so, I was able to enjoy the exercise and the weather. My heart was pounding, but not uncomfortably. I was still able to keep my breathing regular, and I was enjoying the scenery of the city.

Then a shape nearly crashed into me from the side. Chelsea was absolutely dripping with sweat, hunched slightly to one side, and panting like she was on the verge of suffocation. She hobbled beside me with a wild grin. "Thought you lost me, huh?"

I laughed. "What did you do, take a shortcut?"

"What? No. I was—" She bent down to her knees, gasping. She held up one palm as if hoping I'd stop and let her finish.

I felt a little guilty about it, but I kept running. This time, I made it down through the historic waterside section of the city. I looped back toward the hotel and had almost forgotten to wonder what Chelsea was doing until I saw her walking ahead of me with her hands on her hips. She was taking short, staggering steps and her head was rolling around like she was on the verge of passing out. When she turned and saw me coming, she jerked into a jogging motion.

She was half-dragging one leg behind her and hitching with every motion, like both her sides were cramped and one leg had given out on her.

We were only a quarter of a mile or so from the hotel, so I decided to stop at her side. I briefly debated whether touching her would be a bad idea, then decided she was going to fall without my help.

"Jesus," I said, chuckling despite trying not to. "You're going to kill yourself. Here—" I slid my arm around her side, and she melted into my shoulder.

"Beat you here," she gasped.

I grinned. From where she'd hunched over several miles back to where she was now, it was more likely she'd been walking ever since and only covered a few blocks. None of that was important, so I decided to ignore it.

"You need some water. Maybe a sports drink. And some food."

"What makes you say that?" she said, words slurring slightly.

"The fact that you look dehydrated. Come on."

I took her to the room and set her down with a bottle of water while I went to the lobby to get more supplies. I scavenged up an ice pack, some crackers, and an assortment of sports drinks since I wasn't sure what color she preferred. I also placed a room service order for a few sandwiches.

I found her face down on the bed when I reached the room. Her sweat soaked top was on the floor beside her, leaving her just in a black sports bra and neon blue leggings.

I wasn't proud of myself for it, but I stopped for a full two seconds and devoured the sight of her ass. I knew she desperately needed some nutrition, so I controlled the primal urge to pretend I wasn't her boss just for long enough to fuck her brains out in the shower.

"Here. Drink some of this."

She rolled over and sat up a little groggily. I didn't succeed in keeping my eyes off her cleavage, which was glistening with sweat and begging to be touched. Her nipples were even creating two hard, tantalizing peaks through her sports bra. She had no idea what she was doing to me, and I hated that I was so damn thirsty for her. Staying away from relationships and sex had proven to be no problem. Until now. Until Chelsea.

"Is this every color they had?" she asked.

"Why, did I not get the one you like?"

"I'm just wondering why you got so many."

'Because I imagined you might complain if I didn't get the color you wanted."

I sat down beside her and held a red drink toward her. "Am I right?"

Chelsea surprised me by leaning her head on my shoulder. I was still hot and sweating from my run, and something about the heat of our bodies mingling was excruciatingly sexy. I imagined how she'd feel scorching against me if I pinned her down on the bed and took her from above.

"Purple is my favorite." She snatched one from the small collection I'd dropped on the bed and took a few greedy sips. She let out a moan of bliss that made my cock twitch.

"I've never met someone so stubborn, you know."

Chelsea laughed softly. "I'll admit it has been a little bit since my last jog. Okay. A lot of bit."

I moved to the armchair across from the bed where she sat and sank into it. I needed space. Dangerous ideas were bubbling up in my head, and it was only a matter of time before I did something stupid with her sitting that close. I needed to make her talk about something, *anything*. "What's your story, exactly?"

She'd been sipping her drink but paused mid-drink. "You're actually asking about me?"

I shrugged. "I'm curious what kind of situation creates someone like you."

Chelsea smiled a little ruefully, and I noticed she wasn't just looking better after some hydration—she was looking painfully good. She was sprawled comfortably on the bed with her legs slightly spread and her arms planted behind her. Little rivulets of sweat ran from her neck to slide over her clavicle, drawing my eyes.

"It's not much of a story."

"Try me," I said.

"My brother got into trouble when we were in high school. He's a couple years older, and my parents thought he was old enough to kick him out. I disagreed with them."

"That's it?"

"I mean, no. They stopped paying for my tennis lessons, stripped everything from my life I cared about one thing at a time, and eventually kicked me out, too. That was about four years before we... Met."

My dick stirred. Met was a delicate way of putting it. The heat behind her eyes told me she remembered every single moment of that encounter, too. "What about tennis? Why were you even trying so hard to get into that meeting in the first place?"

"I was on the bubble. I thought I was good enough to play in some of the big matches, but I kept getting stuck in these satellite tournaments because I didn't have the money to travel to the bigger ones. I thought the Olympics would help me get noticed and maybe sponsored."

I pursed my lips. "Smart. Actually."

"Believe it or not, I'm not the bumbling idiot you seem to make me out to be."

I winced. She was right, of course. I'd hardly given her a chance to show me who she really was. I'd been too busy trying to put my boot on her neck to break her stubborn confidence. "You're not an idiot," I said. "Far from it. That's actually part of why I wanted to bring you on this trip. I wanted to offer you a position as one of my acquisition agents. You'd scout talent and try to bring them under the Rose Athletic Representation umbrella. Your salary wouldn't be what it is now," I added, feeling childish. Of course it wouldn't. I'd offered her an administrative salary to sit at a ridiculous little desk and do busywork for me. And I'd done it because I was too busy being a prick to think straight. "But you'd get a percentage of the cut from any athlete you bring on board. One percent. The agent who takes over gets fourteen.

"In time, you could work your way up to being a full-fledged agent, too. Acquisitions are always the starting block."

The smile she'd worn faded slowly. "I'd need to know a little more."

"Some of our top athletes earn as much as thirty million per year from contracts with their team. That number can explode upwards when sponsorships enter the equation. One percent of sixty million per year, for example, would be six hundred thousand dollars. Chances are, you'd have to start with some smaller fish. Athletes in less popular sports, maybe. But if you bring in a million-dollar athlete, that's ten thousand a year in your pocket. Bring in a handful more, and you get the picture."

"Yes. Yes!" Chelsea hopped up, and this time, I was ready for it. I knew she was going to try to hug me. I stuck out my arm to stop her, but she swatted it to the side and practically jumped on top of me.

I'd been sitting with my legs casually opened, and the way she landed meant she was halfway straddling me. Her body was radiating heat and still slick with sweat, just like mine.

She pulled back from the hug, and her ecstatic smile melted away. Her eyes grew heavy, sliding down to my mouth.

"Chelsea," I said. "I'd be no good for you."

"I know," she whispered. "I'm only ever drawn to the bad ones. I should've learned my lesson by now. *But I haven't.*" She pulled her lower lip in between her teeth, still fixated on my lips.

"I'm your boss. I'd end up breaking your heart, too."

"Maybe my heart isn't as fragile as you think."

"You work for me. We can't."

"We're adults. You own the entire company. Who is it you're afraid of upsetting?"

"You," I said. A little stab of electricity ran through me when I realized how sincerely I meant that. I didn't want to hurt Chelsea. I'd wanted to prove a point to her, antagonize her, and ultimately drive her to quit. But I didn't want to hurt her. In a way, everything I'd been trying to do might have been driven by the idea that the safest place for her was away from me. The more firmly I could drive her away, the safer she'd be.

"I'm a big girl. I can handle you."

"I've got issues. Scars. Shit you shouldn't have to deal with."

"Are we getting married, or getting ready to have a little fun?" She was breathing hard, and I couldn't ignore the way her breasts were pressing against my chest with a pleasant weight and softness.

At that moment, I think her argument could've been as compelling as, "you put big stick in little hole," and I would've caved. I wanted her. *Fuck*, I wanted her.

I was sliding my hand down the curve of her hip before I'd consciously decided anything. That first touch undid me. It obliterated any good sense or thoughts of restraint. I needed her. I needed to bury myself in her so fucking deep that it hurt.

Chelsea let out a small noise and lowered herself down on my erection. I closed my eyes, pressing my head back into the chair and let her.

There'd be hell to pay for this later, I suspected. But right now, I couldn't make myself stop if I tried.

I was done pretending I hadn't wanted to fuck her since the moment I saw her walk back into my life.

I stood, holding her by her ass as I walked her over to the bed. She tightened her legs around my waist with her hands threaded behind my neck. There was uncertainty in her eyes. Fear, maybe.

"I don't know where we go from here," I said. "But I'm going to explode if I don't get inside you. I want you too damn much."

Chelsea nodded. "No attachments. Just sex."

She was right, of course. The more impersonal we made this, the better it was. For both of us.

"I want you to clean me off first, though," she added, biting her lip. "In the shower."

I grinned. I wasn't about to admit that I'd been filthily looking forward to sweaty, hot sex with her the way she was right this moment. Still, taking her to the shower first would drag things out. I had no idea if I'd ever get to lay my hands on her again, so I'd take every last detour I possibly could.

I tossed her on the bed roughly, then stepped back to strip out of my shirt. She lay there with her legs still spread and her eyes devouring my torso. I grinned down at her, then pulled off my running shorts, letting her get a healthy view of my cock, which was hard enough now to hammer through diamonds

"There's something I need to tell you. Before we—"

I shook my head, then bent down over her to press my hand to her mouth. "You don't get to speak anymore. Until this is over, you're mine. Every inch of you belongs to me until we leave this room. You're my fucking toy, and I'm about to play the shit out of you."

Chelsea's eyes widened. "For some reason," she whispered. "I can't really picture you being the type to play with toys."

I wanted to sigh. Of course she couldn't leave her personality at the door, even for this.

22

CHELSEA

Oh, shit.

I knew what this was. It was the moment before a tsunami. The water had receded, and I was one of the poor fools who walked out to the beach to get a closer look.

Why was the water so far from shore? Wasn't that funny? Oh, what's that giant, life-shattering wave coming toward me at blinding speed? And why does it have abs covered in glistening sweat and a sexy little script tattoo stretching down the side of its rippled torso?

Damon was the tsunami about to crash into me. He was cocked and loaded in both senses of the phrase, and there was no use running now. You didn't outrun moments like this. You didn't outrun *men* like this.

"Stand," Damon said.

It was like the word itself compelled me to my feet. I was standing in front of him now.

Some people probably would've felt embarrassed. After all, Damon could've been carved as a statue of what the gods themselves aspired to.

But me? I decided if *that* man was looking at me the way he was, then I had nothing to be ashamed of. It was a powerful feeling, and every moment his eyes dug into me felt like it pumped energizing, white light straight into my veins.

I felt sexy.

I felt powerful.

I chewed my lip, then met his eyes to wait for his next command.

"Take off your clothes. Slowly. I want you to tease me."

Damon, you kinky bastard.

I used just my index finger to slip the strap of my sports bra to the side, loving how his eyes followed my every movement with obvious hunger.

I realized with a little annoyance that I couldn't sexily shimmy my sports bra down, so I had to try to do a recovery move where I tucked my arm under on the other side and then pulled it over my head.

Of course, being the klutz I was, I managed to slingshot it from the back of my head and straight to Damon.

He caught it in his hand, then lifted it to his nose and *sniffed*.

I couldn't help bulging my eyes. Okay. He wasn't just a kinky bastard. He was a freak. A spectacular, gorgeous, breathtaking freak. And he was sniffing my sports bra.

He clutched it in his fist, then tossed it on top of his suitcase like he was saving it as a trophy. Then he beckoned me closer with one finger.

Dutifully, I walked toward him. I felt like a goddess. Like sex personified. I was the *effing* seductress. I was the siren in the sea, the one who was driving him wild with lust, and I was loving every moment of it.

He took a hard handful of my breasts. Damon sucked in a quick breath, then ran his thumb teasingly across my nipple.

His hands on me were everything. They were atomic. I had to close my eyes and lean into him to stop my now jelly-weak knees from giving out.

"Pants," Damon commanded while still groping my chest.

I shimmied out of my leggings with as much dignity as I could manage. It seemed he was too busy with my boobs to sniff those, I noted with amusement. Or maybe his freakiness had limits.

He cupped me between the legs before I could take off my panties, driving me backwards toward the bed.

I melted against his touch, eyelids fluttering. "You are still supposed to clean me off first, remember?"

Damon growled. He actually growled, then he scooped me up and carried me to the bathroom. He made me feel small and weightless against his huge frame.

Holding me to him with one hand, Damon reached into the shower and turned on the water. He set me down on my feet and pushed my backside against the tall glass frame of the shower.

He looked possessed. None of the reserved, grumpy distance was there. The only thing I saw in his eyes was need, and I found myself desperately wanting to fill that need. I just had to try not to think about how I was undoubtedly setting myself up for disappointment. This was going to be a one-time thing. A one off. I had to believe that, because believing anything else would be naïve.

"Why are your panties still on?" Damon asked between kisses he planted on my neck. Apparently, he had no issue with the fact that I was a sweaty mess. Combined with the whole sports bra sniffing thing, I found it hot in an animalistic sort of way.

"Because you started grabbing my pussy and then picked me up before I could take them off?"

"Smartass," he said, cupping my chin. He studied my lips, then took them in his, greedily kissing me.

I let my eyelids slide shut and fell into the kiss. It was like floating in a dark sky full of bursting fireworks. I could practically see the brightly colored smoke drifting around us, feel the thump of the explosions in the heavy beats of my heart.

It was right.

It was perfect.

It was everything.

And it couldn't last.

Stop thinking like that, Chelsea. I kissed him back, wishing all the glowy warmth in my stomach would stop sending stupid ideas to my brain. Just sex. It was just sex. If I played that on repeat enough times, I could make it true.

He kiss-walked me backward into the water, even though I still had my underwear on. Hot, steaming water splashed over his shoulders to puddle between our joined chests.

"I don't want to get hurt," I said quietly, words lost in the hiss of the shower head.

I shoved my doubts into a deep, dark closet and kissed him again. I reached between his legs and gripped his impossibly thick length. It seemed even bigger than I remembered, and God knew I'd remembered it being big.

"Don't put this in me until we're out of the shower and you're wearing a rubber, okay?" I said. *A rubber I'm going to carefully inspect for holes, this time.*

"Bossy," Damon noted just before he took my shoulders and pushed me up against the wall. He held me there with a hand between my breasts, then reached for a bar of soap with his other hand. With a one handed, careful motion, he lathered up and set the bar down.

For the next several minutes, I received the most thorough cleaning any woman has ever received. He slid his soapy hand across my breasts and nipples, drawing gasps from me at almost every caress. He tenderly cleaned my armpits, even when it made me giggle. He moved his hand across my ass, taking himself a generous tour of *every* available crevice. He also apparently was highly concerned that my clit received a thorough cleaning. What a gentleman.

He took his time, and I couldn't help feeling like it was the most heartbreakingly loving and tender experience of my sexual life. I wasn't sure if that was sad, or just a testament to how wildly out of control my physical feelings toward Damon were becoming.

I'd never been much of a blowjob type of person, but I'd also never considered a cock beautiful before now.

Damon's cock was the Magic Mike of cocks. It worked out, probably had a nightly skincare routine, and looked like it liked all the same movies and shows as me. It was a cock to write love stories about, *or*... Maybe just a cock I really wanted in my mouth.

He chuckled. "Hungry?"

"Starting to be." I slowly got to my knees. Damon's cock twitched in anticipation.

I wrapped my hands around it, noting there was plenty of room for both of them as well as my mouth.

I kissed up his shaft, caressing him with my hands as I did. He moved to lean against the wall. With his head tilted back, he took a handful of my hair. "Fuck, yeah. That's good."

"Just good?" I asked. I plunged my head down on him, cupping his velvety head with my tongue and then swirling as my hands pumped in unison.

He let out a satisfied moan. "You feel so fucking good."

I'd only been doing my thing for a minute or two before he gripped my hair and started using my mouth. He pumped himself into me with wild hunger, but still not roughly in a way that made me feel like I was suffocating or about to gag.

His body started to tense, and I wondered if he was about to spend himself in my mouth. But he pulled back, leaving me to gasp for breath as the head of his penis pulsed inches from my mouth.

"I need to be inside you. Now."

"Condom," I said, standing up. "Also, you were technically just inside me. Kind of silly to pull yourself out of me and say something like that."

"I want your pussy."

"Right," I said a little sheepishly. I'd been joking, obviously, but apparently Damon was too focused to take the hint.

He shut off the water, then carried me to the bed without even drying me off. I flopped down on the sheets, immediately feeling the water on my body start to create a wet patch.

Damon towered over me, regal and proud even in complete nudity.

"It's just sex," I said when our eyes met.

He finished putting a condom on himself and nodded. "Yeah. I know."

I nodded too. Except I wasn't so sure I believed it, even though I knew I needed to. "Are there any holes in that?" I asked.

"What?"

"The condom." I pointed to his rubber-clad dick.

Damon frowned, then did a brief inspection. "No."

Good enough.

He climbed on top of the bed, his rigid body over mine. As he moved himself into position, his erection slid between my legs so that it pressed up against me.

A satisfied gasp slipped from my lips. I found myself lifting my hips to seek out the friction of his length against my folds.

Damon obliged, rocking his hips into mine so that his cock slid along me, gathering my arousal until I could hear the wet sound of our movement.

I was gasping already, and it couldn't have been more than a few seconds. One of his hands gripped my breast almost hard enough to hurt and the other was behind me squeezing my ass up into himself.

God, it felt too good to be safe.

Just when the sensations were reaching a crescendo, he angled his body and with a single motion, he stopped sliding along my pussy and slipped into my entrance.

I reached across his broad back, squeezing him tight. He was so warm and hard. There was a sensation of inevitability somehow—like Damon was more machine than man in this moment, and I'd set something into motion that I couldn't dream of stopping.

Maybe that should've scared me, but all I felt was fascination.

He was big, and still bigger than I remembered. I didn't care what people wanted to believe about childbirth stretching women out down there. Because either I'd gotten tighter—thank you Kegel exercises—or he'd gotten bigger.

I was desperate to be full with him, like the emptiness inside me was suddenly offensive. I needed every inch he could give. "I want all of it," I whispered.

"You can't handle all of it."

"Try me."

Damon grunted, pressing himself harder against me. I felt him slide deeper than I thought he could go.

I squeezed him tighter, breathing hard. "Fuck me. Please."

My words lit some kind of fuse in him, and everything went into overdrive. He gripped me tighter, moved faster, kissed me more fiercely.

Nothing about it was calculated.

I wasn't the latest in his line of conquests. I wasn't getting a clinical trial in the art of perfect sex.

I was getting him.

Damon.

I was getting my first real glimpse at *him*. Damon wanted this, and he wasn't hiding from it. He was embracing it.

I cried out when a sudden orgasm split me through my core. One minute, I'd been thinking about how good he felt and looked as he drove himself into me again and again, the next my eyes were rolling back and I was gasping for breath.

He entwined his fingers with mine above my head. Damon kissed my neck, then my mouth. His pace slowed, and our eyes met.

This wasn't just sex anymore.

He slid into me. Out. In.

It was wet, warm, and absofuckinglutely glorious.

I reached one hand up and felt his lower lip with the pad of my thumb.

He kissed my finger, then my palm, grinning even as he drove me closer to another orgasm.

It was just sex. Just sex. Nothing personal. Nothing real.

Damon's hand made a path up from my shoulder to my cheek. His eyes burned into mine and his brows creased. I could feel him tensing—nearing his own climax.

I arched my body into him, driving him deeper as much as I could from below his body.

"You feel so good," I gasped.

Damon's eyes twitched shut and I felt his cock pulse inside me. He braced himself against the bed and finally collapsed when he was done. I was surprised when his hand slid between my legs. He was still inside me and on top of me, but he moved his hand down to my clit and started rubbing me there. "Come for me, Chelsea. I want you to come all over my cock."

"I already did," I said, smirking.

"Then do it again."

It only took another minute for me to follow his command, and it was several more minutes before he rolled off me.

"That was just sex," he said quietly.

"Yeah," I said. "It was definitely just sex."

I couldn't help thinking about how as we both lay there on our backs, staring at the ceiling, we were giving new meaning to the term "lying on your back."

Shit. I was in trouble. Deep, deep trouble.

23

DAMON

Fuck.

Of all the worlds in the English language, I wasn't sure if any summed up my situation more accurately.

I'd had it figured out just fine. Life. The secrets of the universe. Existence.

I'd figured every damn thing out.

The secret to the game was that you didn't play. Happiness? No. People who chased happiness were only inviting pain. If you weren't greedy, you could settle for a perfect neutral existence. Wake up, work, rinse repeat. No drama, no problems.

But there she was. The wrinkle in my perfectly boring, sterile life. And she was currently sitting across from me with a sandwich the size of her head in her hands. She twisted it one way, then another, as if trying to decide how to avoid getting condiments all over her face. With a little shrug, she decided to dive in, messiness be damned.

I prodded at my burger, feeling like I'd lost my appetite.

What the hell was I doing?

First, I'd offered her a position as an acquisition agent. It was clearly a step in the wrong direction if my plan was to fire her.

And if I wanted to ever experience the absolutely mind-blowing sex we'd had last night again, she couldn't be my employee.

Or could she?

No, dumbass. Not if I didn't want Trish 2.0. Not if I wanted to avoid potential lawsuits and the possibility of undermining the respect my employees had for me. I supposed you could make an argument that they feared me more than they respected me, but it was irrelevant.

I knew the smart thing to do, but my cock was determined to drive me the wrong way down a one-way street. Worse, I'd felt a stirring somewhere else last night.

It was only a hook-up. Just physicality. And yet no matter how much I wanted that to be true, I knew something had shaken loose in my chest when I looked into her eyes. Like an old rusted out truck in a field that had been kicked in just the right place. I never thought it'd run again, but the spark plug had revved up the old, forgotten engine in my core. Now all I could do was question why I wanted to fight it so hard, other than the obvious complication of her being my employee. Other than Trish.

"You want to trade or something?" Chelsea asked. She gestured her gnawed at sandwich toward me, which was dripping mayo-soaked lettuce on her plate.

"Considering you ate your way in from the edges to the center, I'll pass."

She shrugged. "I like to save the best bite for last." Chelsea pointed to a chunk of thick bacon. "That bad boy is going to be worth the wait."

I grinned. I'd never put too much thought into eating. Apparently, Chelsea had strategies for how she attacked her meals. Of course she did.

"About last night..." I looked up, not sure where I was going but knowing I needed to say something.

"It was just what it was," Chelsea said. She took a heaping bite of her sandwich, speaking around the food. "We're adults, right? We can still be professional."

"Yeah, right."

"So you still haven't even told me why we're in Savannah."

"We're going to wine and dine an athlete tonight. Trevor Castle. Have you heard of him?"

She set her sandwich down, dusted off her hands, and gave me a dry look. "Have I heard of the best new tennis player since Federer? *No.* Doesn't ring a bell."

She dropped the act and clapped her hands together then let out a little squeal. "Does this mean we're meeting Trevor tonight?"

Until that exact moment, it had. Now I was second guessing myself. I hadn't considered Chelsea's past as a tennis player. I also hadn't thought too hard about Trevor's playboy status. He was single, and rumor was that he left a trail of satisfied women in every city he passed through.

Rumor also had it that he was being courted for acquisition by none other than my ex-girlfriend, Trish. *And no,* that fact had nothing to do with me trying to land him for Rose Athletic.

"I was going to have you stay at the hotel, actually," I said.

Chelsea glared. "What? You just told me I'm going to be doing real work. Shouldn't I be tagging along to see how the master himself does it?"

Annoyingly, she had a point. "I'll consider it. But you would need to dress for fine dining if you planned to come. I'm guessing you didn't pack anything appropriate."

Chelsea's eyes could've set a large pot of water to boil in seconds. "Considering my lovely boss didn't tell me anything about fine dining... No. I didn't."

I hated how weak I was becoming for her. Just a few days ago, I would've grinned and taken it as an easy out. Problem solved.

Now, all I could think about was how badly she seemed to want to prove herself. I'd begun to paint the picture of her past.

Of how she'd been sidelined when her real opportunity to chase her dream had come. Some asshole had knocked her up and left her to clean up the mess, and I still had no idea who or why. Asking her now would've only complicated things more, so I kept my mouth shut on it.

I did know I was going to hate myself if I was part of shutting down her next dream, as ridiculously sentimental as that was. "We have a few hours. You can take one of my company cards and go find something appropriate."

She waited. "That's all? How much am I allowed to spend? Where is this dinner, exactly?"

"Frankly, I don't care. But you're representing Rose Athletic. Your first lesson in acquisitions is to look the part. Athletes can sniff out incompetence from a mile away. You need to look like money, so they'll believe you're already making it."

"Would you come with me and help me pick?"

"You think I don't have anything better to do?"

She paused for a long moment, cheeks reddening. "You could come into the changing rooms with me."

Fucking hell. There was no way I could agree to that. Absolutely not.

I FOLLOWED CHELSEA INTO THE CHANGING ROOM AT A FANCY LITTLE designer boutique on Main Street. My dick was already pathetically hard, and the way she was shyly sneaking looks at me was only making it worse.

"This is a terrible idea," I said quietly. There was a small army of women outside the fitting rooms waiting to give Chelsea more dresses to try. At least that would stop me from getting any ideas about taking things further.

"You don't like the green?" she held up the dress and worked her lips to the side. "I think it's nice."

"I'm sure the dress will be fine. I'm talking about this. *Us.*"

"Wow. Already graduating to 'us?' Do you normally fall head over heels this quickly?"

"Chelsea. I'm being serious."

"I know. You always are." Without a moment's hesitation, she slipped out of the skirt she'd been wearing.

My already hard dick went so stiff it hurt when I saw the black lace panties she was wearing. I sucked in air through my nose, trying to calm myself.

Chelsea caught my eye, then flashed the sexiest fucking smirk I'd ever seen. She pulled her shirt over her head, and I couldn't take it anymore.

I pressed my palm between her legs and kissed her neck. I felt the damp heat of her pussy. She was as turned on as I was, and it only made me want her more. "You're so fucking wet for me," I growled into her ear.

"That was for someone else."

I grinned at her. It was the exact line she'd used five years ago. "You're still a bad liar."

Chelsea's breath shuddered when I pushed her panties aside and dipped my fingers inside her. Her walls gripped me tauntingly. I nearly pulled my cock out and took what I wanted, but I heard footsteps approaching the small fitting room.

"How's it looking?"

"Hot," I said.

The girl laughed. "Sounds like he's enjoying the view."

"You could say that," Chelsea managed with three of my fingers inside her. "I might just need a minute. It's a tight fit."

"She's right," I added.

"Oh. Okay," the girl said. She sounded cheerily unaware of what we were doing. "I'll check back on you two lovebirds in a little. It's so cute when boyfriends want to be in the dressing room."

"Boyfriend," Chelsea mouthed, wiggling her eyebrows.

"Don't get any ideas."

She looked between her legs where I was still knuckle deep in her pussy. "Do as you say, not as you do?"

I grimaced, then pulled my hand out of her. Without looking away from her, I brought my fingers to my mouth and licked them clean. "Yeah. Something like that."

Chelsea shivered, then let out a breath she'd apparently been holding. "Maybe I should actually try this on?"

"Probably." My phone buzzed in my pocket. I glanced at it and felt my blood run cold when I saw the name.

Trish: **Heard you're in Savannah today. You wouldn't happen to be trying to steal Trevor Castle from under my nose, would you?**

I shoved my phone back in my pocket. Chelsea was watching me with furrowed eyebrows. "Everything okay?"

"It's fine," I snapped.

She looked like she wanted to ask more, but she quietly slipped on the dress, and neither of us brought it up again.

But I couldn't quite get it out of my head. Trish was probably here. In Savannah. What would she do if I landed Trevor's contract, anyway? Follow through on her threats from when she left?

Part of me almost wanted to. Part of me was so damn tired of letting her hold it over my head.

I decided to enjoy the moment I was in; not whatever cold hell Trish might bring on me down the line. I currently had an unfiltered view of Chelsea's ass and the tight little mound of her pussy against her panties as she bent down to pick up the next dress in line.

Yeah. I could get used to looking at that.

24

CHELSEA

Trevor Castle was the new king of the tennis world. I'd seen his matches on TV and his highlights on the sports channels. Even though I'd already brushed shoulders with a few incredibly famous names, including Damon's own brother, Chris, this was different.

I'd idolized Trevor, even back when I was fifteen and hearing stories of the high school kid who was already cracking his way into the top ranks of the USTA. I'd admittedly had a small crush on him back then, too, but so did every other girl with a functioning reproductive system.

And now I was sitting with him and Damon Rose at a white tablecloth dining table. We'd been given the solitary table on a roof side balcony with beautiful stonework and candles. Gentle music trickled out the French doors from the dining room, and the air was saturated with the scent of melted butter and herbs.

I was salivating, and I wasn't sure if it was entirely because of the food.

Trevor joined us a little late, which meant I'd got to sit in tense silence with Damon for several minutes while we waited. I wasn't sure if he was pissed that I'd insisted on coming, or if he was jealous. He might've even been dwelling on whatever that message on his phone had been. Ever since he'd glanced at his phone in the changing room, he'd been in a dark mood—even by Damon standards.

I'd been chipping away at my resolution to stay detached since last night. Step one was when his penis arrived on the scene. Step two was when he practically made my heart explode —against its better judgment, for the record. It wasn't anything he said in particular, but it was in the subtle change I'd been sensing. Damon was softening toward me. He was opening up in his own way, and I knew enough to know that made me different than everyone else with him. It made me special.

It also forced me to face the fact that I needed to find a way to tell him about Luna. When Damon was the grumpy bosshole with no heart, I hardly felt guilty for keeping the secret. Now, things were changing so quickly it already felt like I'd waited too long. Five years too long.

"You okay?" Trevor asked. He casually popped a chunk of bread in his mouth and chewed, watching me closely.

Trevor was dusty blond haired, clean shaven, young, and covered in lithe muscle. He was beautiful, but in an entirely different way than Damon. Trevor had easy looks. They were the kind you could trust—at least for a fling. He was the prototypical hook-up guy. Too wild and free to tie down, but too good natured to mistrust.

Then there was Damon. I looked at him again as he brooded across from Trevor. He'd dressed in a sharp suit that highlighted all the serious edges he had. Damon was rugged and coarse. He was dark and confusing.

If the two of them were movies, Trevor was the blockbuster hit that you'd probably forget a week after watching it, even though you enjoyed the ride. Damon was the indie flick loaded with enough twists and turns to keep it in your head forever.

"I'm great, yeah," I said. *Prove to Damon that you can do a good job at this. Be personable. Win him over.* "I saw your match last weekend. That comeback was incredible. It might've been the most amazing thing I've seen on a court all year."

I couldn't quite tell from the corner of my view, but I was almost certain Damon rolled his eyes.

"Thanks," Trevor flashed a confident smile. "Truth was I was shitting myself the whole time. Gerard has always had my number, especially on clay."

I nodded. "But you still have the edge on him historically. Last time I looked you led him by what was it, twenty wins?"

Trevor hooked his thumb toward me while looking at Damon. "I see you brought in an expert. I'm impressed."

Damon, always the serious grump, nodded as if this was exactly what he'd planned. "Chelsea used to play herself. Not at your level, of course, but—"

"Oh, I know. I recognize her. We played against her in a mixed doubles tournament when she was in college. I still remember that wicked kick serve you had, Chels."

Chels? I couldn't quite believe Trevor Castle was giving me a nickname. I didn't know if I should be annoyed or flattered. I *did* know what Damon thought of it.

He was leaning forward so the vein on the side of his head was visible, fists clenched on his fork and knife. He looked like a caveman about to bang the table and demand food.

I wanted to laugh but didn't want to antagonize him. Did I find guilty pleasure in seeing him squirm? Yes. Did I want to intentionally fuel the fire? No. I wasn't cruel, unlike some people.

"We're prepared to make an offer," Damon said.

I shot him a look. So much for being a smooth negotiator.

Trevor popped another bite of bread into his mouth, chewing between perfect, ivory white teeth. "I'm here, so I'm obviously considering. Although I've got a meeting with Trish Jameson tomorrow, too. But I'm done with Dwight. That much is for sure.

He really fucked the pooch with my sponsors. How would you have handled it better?"

Damon launched into a discussion that went back and forth until we'd reached dessert. I was taking as many mental notes as I could.

I gradually realized Damon's negotiation technique was about pure confidence. He didn't bullshit. He didn't sugarcoat. There were no sales pitches or corny lines. He simply laid out the facts, and the facts were that he had a track record of success. Massive success, at that.

I could tell Trevor was convinced before we even got our entrees, but he also impressed me with the depth of questions he'd prepared to ask Damon. He clearly didn't want to be saddled with another sub-par agent again.

I had to pee. Badly. I'd been draining waters since we sat down, partly out of nervousness. I didn't want to embarrass Damon by excusing myself in the middle of the meeting, but enough was enough.

"Sorry, I've got to use the restroom," I said.

Trevor and Damon continued their conversations, both barely touching their dessert.

On my way out of the bathroom, a woman I recognized but couldn't immediately place stopped me. "You must be Chelsea."

I squinted. *Oh, shit.* I recognized her because I'd spent a solid chunk of time internet stalking her. Trish Jameson. "You're Trish," I said, not bothering to pretend I didn't know who she was.

She looked exactly like her pictures, except taller. She was wearing some expensive checker patterned dress and a huge pair of diamond earrings. "I happened to be eating here when I noticed you and Damon were wining and dining my client."

"Trevor hasn't decided on a new agent yet."

Trish sniffed dismissively. "He's mine, and it looks like I need to remind Damon that he's my bitch."

"*Excuse me?*" I didn't expect the rush of anger I felt to hear her say that. *Her bitch?* Who was this woman?

Trish gave a smug wiggle of her shoulders. "Maybe you should ask him about it. I'm sure he'll tuck his tail between his legs and dodge your questions. Try it, sweetheart. Oh, and if you haven't already, don't let him put his cock in you. You have no idea where it's been."

I stood there frozen in rage for too long to actually do anything. All I managed was to run through a few imaginary scenarios where I grabbed wine glasses or plates of food and tossed them on her stupid face. Except I was too slow, so she was gone by the time I snapped back to reality and realized I still had to pee. *Badly.*

When I came back out of the bathroom, Trevor was leaning against the wall of the small bathroom hallway, apparently waiting for me.

"Hey," he said, flashing a crooked smile.

Jesus. Does anyone else want to bump into me while I'm up from the table?

"Uh, hi."

"Once you're off the clock, maybe we could grab drinks."

"Oh. I'm flattered, but I—"

Before I knew what was happening, Damon was standing between us. He hadn't put a hand on Trevor, but I could see his knuckles were white and his jaw was clenched.

"Can my employee leave the restroom in peace?" he asked after a tense moment of silence.

Trevor pulled a face. Damon might've just undone all the good rapport they'd built, if the expression he wore was any indication. "Yeah, man. Didn't realize you two were a thing. Is that how you run things at Rose Athletic? You bring a little sex buddy on all your work trips, or—"

Now Damon's hands were on Trevor's shoulders. He had him pinned against the wall. "Careful."

"You'll wish you were," Trevor said. "We're done here."

"Are we?" Damon asked.

"Yes," I said firmly. "Let him go."

Damon grudgingly obliged.

Trevor dusted off his jacket, then shook his head. "Fucking waste of time."

Once he left, I turned to Damon. We had relative privacy in the small hallway leading to the bathrooms, so I didn't have to worry about spectators.

"What the hell was that?" I asked. "I don't need a caveman to bash anyone who looks at me over the head. You just embarrassed us both."

"That was me wanting you. For myself. All to my goddamn self, okay? Is that what you want to hear? I tried not to, but I can't stop thinking about you. Wanting you. Remembering the way you taste. You're addictive, and I spent five years trying to convince myself I wasn't addicted to something I'd never get my hands on again. And now..."

I gripped his jacket and pulled him in, kissing him on the mouth. He kissed me back slowly and tenderly.

"I'm still pissed at you, for a lot of things," I said. "But yeah. *Okay.* It's possible I feel some of what you're talking about, too."

"Good. Because I don't know what I'd do if I couldn't have more of you."

"Damon... Trish was here. She stopped me on the way into the restroom. She said something weird about how you were her 'bitch.' What is she talking about?"

I hadn't realized it until the words left me, but it felt like a test. If Damon could finally trust me and open up, maybe I could tell him the truth about Luna. *God.* I still dreaded that conversation, because I knew I wasn't completely in the right for keeping the truth from him. Then again, I was willing to be wrong to protect Luna, and that was what it always kept coming back to.

Damon shook his head. "Trish will say anything she can to fuck with me. That's all."

"Damon..."

"That's all," he said again, more firmly.

And just like that, I felt my resolution to tell him about Luna slip away once again.

25

DAMON

It was Sunday, and that meant Chelsea and I were still booked in the same hotel room for one more day. After the disaster of a dinner with Trevor and the quick conversation that made Chelsea go mute on me afterwards, we'd slept separately and barely spoken.

I woke before the sun rose, but I already heard the shower running. The door was closed, and I had no doubt it was locked.

We'd been on the brink of something, but it felt like everything split apart in a single moment last night. She wanted to know what Trish was talking about, and I didn't want to say.

Was that all it took? Was everything between us really so fragile?

I threw on some clothes, smoothed my bed-messed hair with my hands, and headed out from our hotel room. I needed to talk to Trish.

I sent her a text telling her to meet me at a breakfast place not far from my hotel. I had no idea if she'd show, so I got seated in the corner and ordered some eggs and coffee while I waited.

It hadn't even been fifteen minutes before Trish entered. It was early as hell, but she already looked like she'd spent hours applying makeup and fussing with her hair. I remembered how that had driven me crazy when I was with her. She'd been pretty without all the fuss, but she insisted on dumping hours in front of the mirror every day. It made me think about how Chelsea barely wore any makeup. I was no expert, but as far as I could tell, she just wore a little eyeliner. I was sure she probably used some other mysterious, womanly tools of beautification, but it couldn't have been much.

Damn it. I was thinking about her already. Comparing. Torturing myself by thinking about how much better she was than Trish—the one woman I'd been dumb enough to try to love.

Trish undid the button on her cashmere coat, revealing a tight-fitting blue dress that hugged her curves and breasts. She sat down, then folded her hands in front of herself quietly.

"Why are you still fucking with me?" I asked.

"That's why you wanted to meet?" Trish asked. She leaned in her eyes lit with anger. "Did your silly, ridiculously short little blondie get mad after what I said? Is that it?"

I was careful not to let any of my annoyance show. "You got everything you wanted when you left. That was the deal. I let you take what you wanted, and you'd leave."

"Maybe I'm bored of our arrangement. Besides, you knew I was courting Trevor Castle for Jameson Reps. From where I'm sitting, you're the one who started this."

"We're both professionals." *One of us is, at least.* "We're occasionally going to have our eyes on the same athletes. It doesn't need to turn into whatever you're trying to make this."

Trish ran her tongue across her lip, as if considering something. "I want to make us work again."

I had to sit back and replay what she'd just said several times to be sure I'd heard her right. "*What?* You broke things off with *me.* You were very thorough in burning a trail of destruction in your wake, too. Why would I *ever* remotely consider taking you back?"

"Because I get you. I know your soft spots. I know all your secrets, Damon. Blondie doesn't. I could see it in her eyes last night. You haven't even told her as much as you told me. Like it or not, you need me. You were whole when you were with me, and now you're just a shell of who you were."

I shook my head. "I'm not having this conversation with you. And just to be sure we're crystal clear. *No*. In every sense of the word, *no*. You and I will never happen again. So if it's jealousy driving you to try to put a wedge between Chelsea and I, then fuck off."

Trish smiled. "If I can't have you, why should she get you?"

"Trish," I warned.

She got up, then picked up my cup of coffee and sipped. "Mmm. You and I always did like it exactly the same. Didn't we?"

She left the restaurant, and I found myself wondering if I'd just stoked the flames instead of putting them out.

26

CHELSEA

I had trouble sleeping, so I woke up early Sunday morning and showered. When I got up, Damon had been asleep on the couch still, his huge body gently rocking with each breath. I'd guiltily watched him for a while, then reminded myself I needed to keep my guard up. I didn't need to be standing there in the faint light of morning admiring the way the rising sun lit his profile, or how painfully kissable his lips were.

When I got out of the shower, he was gone. I'd been rehearsing what I was going to say while the water poured over me.

You need to learn to trust me, or I won't ever be able to trust you. It's not a one-way street. You can open up to me and I won't hurt you, I promise, but if you don't give me a chance, I can't help.

I'd tried and tried to think of the right words to express all the frustration and confusion I felt, but nothing had seemed right. I eventually decided to just wing it when I got out, but he was gone.

I quickly threw on my clothes. A stupid part of me thought back to last night—to Trish and how supremely confident she'd been. If Damon was really bound to her by something—whether it was blackmail or personal weakness—what would happen if she'd asked him to come over for an early morning booty call?

Stupid. I knew I was being stupid, but one of the worst things about being stupid was self-awareness wasn't always a cure.

I headed outside our hotel and started walking an aimless circle, not even knowing what I was looking for. The only thing I could think of was the offhanded comment Damon had made when I was still keeping pace with him on our jog. He'd grunted that a breakfast place looked good, and it was only a few minutes from our hotel.

I hurried there.

I arrived just in time to see Trish Jameson walking out of the restaurant. She swiveled her head, spotted me, and flashed a huge, predatory smile. "Blondie!" she called from down the street, then walked toward me.

I looked past her through the glass windows of the shop and saw Damon glaring at his plate inside. My insides went icy. Maybe I wasn't as stupid as I thought.

"Oh, don't worry. I haven't fucked him. *Yet,*" Trish said. "Well, I guess that's not accurate. We fucked hundreds of times already, but I mean I haven't had that big, perfect dick of his yet this weekend."

"What were you doing in there together?"

"You want the truth? Because if you ask him, he's just going to give you some bullshit story about what a crazy bitch I am. The truth is he never got over me. He still wants to make things work, and I just might let him. So we were planning a date for tonight. But go ahead, ask him yourself. I'm sure he'll have fun spinning up a lie for you."

I clenched my fists and said nothing as Trish walked away, supremely happy with herself. This was a crossroads point. I sensed that.

My instincts wanted to believe everything she said and go in there guns blazing. I wanted to demand to know how Damon could do this to me, even if we'd never made anything official. We both knew what we felt, and how could he still think about someone else when it felt so right to be together.

But I thought about what that banshee of a woman must've done to him. Whether I knew the details or not, I knew she hurt him. Maybe it still hurt for him. He didn't need me to take her word over his. He didn't need me to doubt him.

And even if trust *was* a two-way street, some people had more reasons to protect their trust than others. So I sucked up all my emotions and walked into the restaurant, then sat across from Damon. He lifted his eyes, saw me, and frowned.

"How'd you find me here?"

"Mild stalker talents," I said dismissively. "But that's not the point. Look… I've been thinking about all this wrong."

Damon set down his fork and gave me his full attention. "What do you mean?"

"I just ran into Trish. *Again.* By the way, she's a raging psychopath. But she keeps trying to convince me you've got some maniacal secret. Or that you two are about to sneak off and sleep together any moment. And I decided I don't care what she says. I don't even care that you are still not ready to open up to me. Someone always has to be the first one to trust, and I'm willing to be the one to put myself out there. So… I trust you."

"Damn it." Damon sighed, folded up his napkin, and threw it on his plate. "You're a pain in my ass, you know that, right?"

"Uh," I said slowly. "I think there must be some kind of miscommunication. I'm trying to say—"

"I know. And stop talking before I change my mind and decide not to tell you this. Trish blackmailed me. I thought I loved her. After you and I met at the Marriott five years ago, I had this emptiness. I tried to fill it with her.

"I ignored the warning signs, and every time I felt like things were strained, I gave her more responsibility and power at the company. Eventually, I told her a few things I never should've told her."

"Such as?" I asked carefully when he didn't continue for a few seconds.

"One was that I faked my certifications in business for the first few years. My brother knew, but none of the other athletes I took on did. I eventually went and got it all taken care of, but there are regulations. If it ever got out and someone investigated properly, I'm not sure what would happen. I do know my credibility would be shot."

"Wow," I said. "And Trish knows?"

"Yeah. She threatened to out me if I didn't let her hand-pick from my clients when she left. The only reason I still have *some* clients is there were a few who refused to leave, even when she hinted that I was a fraud to them."

"You said you told her a few things? What else was there?"

Damon sighed. "I may have admitted what got me into being an agent in the first place. And that I take on many of my clients strictly to help protect them from predatory situations. A lot of the work I personally do involves scouting situations where young athletes are prime targets for relatives and family to take advantage. I try to sign them, regardless of how it stands to benefit Rose Athletic."

"You really do that? But wait, wouldn't that mean you actually have a heart in there somewhere? Because last time I checked, there was just a black ball of grumpy dickweed floating around where it should be."

"Funny. And all it means is I don't like to see people get screwed. *Usually*," he added with a wicked glint in his eyes that I knew was especially for me.

I squirmed a little, but I was still unpacking everything he'd said. "Why would that matter to Trish, though? The fact that you try to help people?"

"She could show potential clients how much resources we're

wasting on athletes who are a step above charity cases. Combined with my fraudulent past and a few other little scandals she knows about, she has me by the balls, more or less."

"She did. But now you have me. And you know what I am?"

"I do. Remember? You're a pain in my ass."

"You might want to get checked out for hemorrhoids with all those ass pains you apparently have. But no, I'm a problem solver."

"Sometimes, the only solution to a problem is to avoid it or endure it."

"Wrong. Just give me a little time, and I'll figure this one out." Except I couldn't help thinking how avoiding and enduring was exactly what I'd been doing when it came to the truth about Luna. I couldn't put it off forever. Sooner rather than later, I needed to tell Damon the truth.

I just had to decide how and when.

27

DAMON

It was evening, and even though I knew I should really be using my time to try to patch things up with Trevor Castle, I could only think about Chelsea.

I'd told her the truth. Instead of making me feel like an idiot, I felt free. I didn't feel vulnerable, I felt as if I'd finally been released from something that had been gripping me too tightly to breathe for years now.

I wasn't dumb, of course. I knew Trish still held enough information to make my business go nuclear right under my nose, and she was apparently dead set on using it against me now. But for the first time, it felt like I had someone in my corner.

We were walking by the waterside. Savannah had a historic section that ran along the river. Cobbled roads led down a strip of shops that were mixed in with scenic overpasses and endless places to sit and admire the views.

Chelsea had taken my hand, and even though I'd always felt like people who held hands in public were obnoxious, I let her. I might've even enjoyed having the soft smallness of her fingers threaded between mine.

We sat down on a bench next to a stone monument. The

water spread out in front of us and an old school, massive paddleboat trundled by while we watched.

"There's something I should've told you a long time ago," Chelsea said. "You have every right to be mad, so, I'm just going to say it."

I braced myself. What the hell was she talking about? Whatever it was, it felt like two cold hands were gripping my insides, threatening to squeeze tight and rip me apart at a moment's notice.

"Five years ago, you got me pregnant. The condom broke, and I never told you. I kept it a secret because I was afraid you'd use your money and influence to make me do something I didn't want to do. Get an abortion, give up the baby—I didn't know. But I thought you were a very bad person. I was ashamed of myself for sleeping with you and for letting something like that happen. I just—"

I realized I hadn't been breathing. I shook my head, sucking in my first breaths. "I wore a condom."

"It broke," she repeated.

I blinked. "You never told me?"

I realized she was already explaining all of this, but she patiently shook her head. "I convinced myself you would hate me for it. That you'd hate the baby, too. I thought everyone would be better off if you never knew. Then I wound up working for you, and I think part of me wanted to reassure myself that I'd made the right call—that you really were the heartless asshole I thought you were back then. But you're not. There's so, *so* much more to you. You deserved to know back then, and you deserve to know now. She's your daughter, Damon."

I leaned forward on my knees. It felt like everything around me was spinning.

A daughter?

I had a fucking daughter?

There were too many emotions churning inside me to count

or identify. It all blurred together in a thumping mass that felt like rushing water in my ears and hoofbeats in my chest. "She's mine?"

"Yes," Chelsea said, smiling as tears twinkled in the corners of her eyes. "And I know you probably hate me now, but I already waited too long to tell you. I just—"

I stood suddenly. "I need some time to think about this."

Chelsea didn't get up or try to stop me. She just nodded, hanging her head. "I understand."

I handed her the hotel key. "I'll have plane tickets sent to your room tomorrow morning."

She looked like she wanted to ask about a dozen questions, but all she did was nod again.

Fuck.

I didn't know how to feel. I really didn't.

28

CHELSEA

Luna hummed as she showed me how she learned to pour her own bowl of cereal while I was gone for the weekend. It was Monday morning. Birds were chirping outside, the sun was shining, and I needed to be at the office in a little less than an hour. I also hadn't heard a word from Damon since our conversation in Savannah, and I'd kept myself up at night worrying he was meeting with teams of lawyers to figure out how to take custody of Luna from me.

Except, I knew that was crazy.

Maybe I'd only *really* known him for a week, but it felt like more. And I couldn't truly make myself believe Damon would do something like that. If I did, I knew I wouldn't have ever told him the truth, no matter how wrong it might've been.

I was stirred from my thoughts when Luna lifted up a milk carton the size of her head. Her eyes were barely over the counter as she stood on her little pink kitty stool and tried to aim the milk into her bowl.

"Oh—" I said, half-reaching for her. "Do you want me to help you?"

Luna grunted with effort, then sloshed about half a gallon of milk in the bowl. It splashed over the side and dripped from the counter to the floor. Unbothered, she set the milk back down with determination in her eyes and her tongue sticking out. She screwed the cap on—which made her shoot me a smug little grin—then scooted it out of her way.

Next, she poured cereal into the bowl until it created a floating mountain of multi-colored sugar balls.

She spread her hands. "Tada!"

"Wow," I said. "That's really impressive. I guess I don't need to help you make your breakfast anymore, huh?" So long as that big money from Rose Athletic actually hits my account this Friday. Otherwise, Luna would run through a month's worth of milk money in three days with pouring skills like that.

There was a knock at the door. My heart sped up. Had Damon come? Was he going to take Luna away? Did he just want to see her?

I pulled open the door and saw Milly. She was already dressed in her tennis skirt and visor, presumably for a morning training session she was on the way to.

"Oh, it's you," I said.

"Nice to see you too." Milly let herself in and set her bag on my coffee table. "I want to know how your weekend went."

Considering the size of my apartment, we'd both gotten used to having our conversations in front of Luna. Thankfully, she was still just young enough to only pick up on bits and pieces, and we didn't need to be *too* careful.

"I told him," I said.

Milly didn't say anything at first, then her eyes went wide. "You told him. Like... you told him, told him?"

"Yeah."

"Did he murder you?"

"Unless this is hell, no. Because I don't think there would be Mondays in Heaven."

She slumped back in the chair. "Wow. What made you do

that? I mean, what about all the things you were worried about before?"

"Do what?" Luna paused with one of the paper dolls I'd made in her hand. "Who is him?"

"Nothing sweetie. We need to go soon though, why don't you go use the bathroom before we head out."

"Okie dokie." Luna hopped down from her chair and headed to the restroom.

I chewed the inside of my mouth. "We might've slept together, too."

Milly made a silent "O" with her mouth. "Girl. You were with the man for two days. Did you also propose?"

"No. But I think I was wrong about him. And I suddenly felt like the shittiest person on Earth for not telling him the truth earlier. I had to."

"Well, what now?"

"Now I show up to work and hope he doesn't toss me out the window."

"Well, what did he say after you told him?"

"Nothing. He just walked off and had plane tickets sent to my room. He hasn't texted, called, or anything."

"Hmm." Milly popped up from the couch. "You'll figure something out. You always do."

I rolled my eyes. "That's not super helpful."

"Is that what you wanted? Practical advice? Because my philosophy is to let my friends vent when they have problems, not give them solutions they'll ignore."

I groaned. "If you've got a solution, I'm all ears."

"You kind of are…" Milly reached for my ear and tugged it. "I've never noticed how big they are."

"Stop," I laughed, slapping her hand away. "This is serious."

"Then just give him time. You gave him a lot to process, and he's probably trying to figure out how he feels. Simple as that."

"Simple as that," I repeated quietly. "Yeah."

"Well!" Milly hiked her bag over her shoulder. "See you later, if he doesn't kill you. Also, you'd better hope he's not venting his anger into another woman's vagina right about now."

A spike of jealousy ran through me. *No.* I didn't believe he'd do that. Not with Tia Klein, not with Trish, and not with any other woman. Despite my best attempts to the contrary, I trusted Damon.

29

DAMON

The door to my office swung open hard enough to bang against the wall. Chris came in looking exhausted, then plopped himself in the chair across from my desk. He was wearing a sleeveless t-shirt that showcased his tattooed arms and gray sweatpants. His hair was a sweaty mess.

"You good?" I asked. "And if the answer is 'no,' I'm going to need you to make it someone else's problem. I have a lot on my mind right now."

Chris considered me. "Do you ever wonder if you've made a mistake?"

I didn't like where this was going. "What did you do?"

My brother sighed. "I mean, nothing, yet. But I'm planning to make a mistake and I was trying to figure out how I'd feel afterwards."

"Have you considered not making this mistake? The one you're planning to make?"

"If that was an option, I wouldn't do it."

"I see. And what am I supposed to do for you here, exactly?"

Chris got up from his chair with another dramatic sigh. "Nothing. I just needed to see your frowning face. Sometimes it wakes me up more than coffee. Like hiding a scary doll under your bed or something."

"You can leave now."

He paused at the door. "I think I figured it out, by the way. You say it like "*wurshur.*" He made a strange face, moving his lips for emphasis. "Wurshur sauce."

"What?"

"Everybody pronounces it like it's this eight-syllable word. *Worcestershire sauce.* But I saw a cooking show and they just said Wurshur sauce." He shrugged. "I also stocked up your fridge with a gallon jug of it. Enough for everyone now."

I gave him an exasperated look, which he grinned at. "See? That's the look. Always wakes me up."

It was only a few minutes later before I saw Chelsea take a seat at her desk in the center of the office floor. Within a few seconds, she'd already looked toward my office about five times.

I watched her with templed fingers. I hadn't handled anything on my agenda for the day, and as another half hour ticked by, I didn't so much as open my email.

I was a father. At least that was her side of the story.

To tell the truth, hearing what she said had brought out the worst in me. It made me wonder if this was her angle the whole time. Get her foot in the door at Rose Athletic. Then claim her kid was mine to extort me.

It was exactly the sort of thing I'd been avoiding relationships for, and the moment I slipped up, here it was.

But she hadn't come to me with any demands. If anything, she looked nervous. Scared, even. Chelsea Cross didn't get scared, as far as I'd seen. She only seemed to exist somewhere on a scale of stubbornness.

I groaned, then left my office to head for her desk.

Daria stopped me before I got there. "Sir," she said. As usual, Daria looked like she was either about to take a nap or she'd just woken from one. "There's... Something interesting waiting for you in the break room."

I frowned. "What is it?"

Daria gave a disinterested shrug. "Wouldn't be very interesting if I told you. Would it?"

I looked to Chelsea, who had been watching *me*. She jerked her head back to her computer.

I moved past Daria to the break room. I tried the door, but it was locked. "What's going on?" I demanded. A couple heads popped up over partitions at the sound of my voice.

There was a click of the lock being released. I turned the handle and pushed the door open. Inside, I was greeted by Tia Klein. She was wearing a tight-fitting dress that was shockingly short. She met my eyes, then gave a sly smile.

"You've been playing hard to get with me, Damon. I figured I'd play hard, too." She reached for the hem of her dress and I could tell she was about to rip it off. I moved forward, putting my hand on hers. "Don't—"

Tia looked unbothered. She fluttered her eyelashes, then kissed me without warning.

I pulled back just in time to see Chelsea standing in the doorway.

"Oh," Chelsea said quietly.

30

CHELSEA

Stupid.

I rushed down the stairs of the building thinking how stupid I'd been.

I heard the door at the top of the stairwell swing open and bang against the wall. "Chelsea!" A deep voice called. "Wait."

I thought about all the times I'd watched in agony as some dumb heroine in a movie ran off instead of standing still for ten seconds to listen. As much as I wanted to be exactly that sort of dumb, I waited with my hand on the knob of the door. Damon came down a few seconds later.

He turned me gently to face him, but I pushed off his hands.

"Hey," he said softly. "She surprised me in there. I had no idea she was going to try to kiss me. I was only standing that close to get her to stop from pulling her dress over her head."

"Is that the truth?"

"Unfortunately."

I frowned. "Why is it unfortunate?"

"Because my life would be a hell of a lot simpler if I wanted to fuck a woman like Tia Klein. Instead, my dumbass only seems to want you."

"Did you just try to romance me while leading with the fact that it'd be better if you wanted to sleep with another woman?"

Damon lifted my chin with his knuckle. "Words were never my strong suit."

"What *is* your specialty, then?"

He took a half step closer. A faint grin curved his lips on one side. "Making you come seems to be a strength of mine."

The man had a point. "How are you with forgiveness?" I asked.

Damon was stroking my hair, and it felt like heaven. "Normally? I'm shit. But once again, you're a pain in my ass. I can't seem to stay mad. Even if you should've told me I got you pregnant. Even if you should've let me help you with money. Even if you made me wait five years to meet my daughter."

"If it makes you feel any better, she was in my stomach for nine months of that. So…"

"Smartass."

I smiled. "What are you going to do about it?"

"Apologize for bailing on you in Savannah. And maybe if you give me a chance, I could give you another demonstration of my strong suit."

"Wait, which one? The one where you make me come, or the one where you are a grumpy asshole?"

"It'll be a surprise."

31

DAMON

Dick swung by the office to take us to Chelsea's apartment. Grant would be there with Luna, and it'd be my first time meeting her as my daughter—not just the kid of the woman I was infatuated with.

Chelsea and I sat in the back seat.

She was watching me extra closely, I noticed. She was also constantly fidgeting with her hands in her lap.

I'd learned a lot about Chelsea lately, and one of those things was how well she hid her real emotions. She was nervous as hell, and she couldn't hide that from me.

She was likely worried I'd disappoint Luna somehow. I could only imagine how nervous she was to see how I'd be around her daughter—*our* daughter. She'd been through hell to protect Luna from me all this time, and now she was putting mountains of trust in me not to fuck it up.

Dick whistled. "The sexual tension back there is through the roof. Smells like prom night at a middle school. Hormones so thick my nose hairs are gonna get singed off."

Chelsea cleared her throat and shifted.

"Richard, I pay you to drive, not for commentary."

"Richard, Richard, Richard," Dick groaned. "What is it, anyway, boss? You afraid to let a little dick touch those lips?"

Chelsea choked on something.

I sighed. "He thinks he's being funny. He wants me to call him Dick instead of Richard."

Dick nodded. "If you ask me, you ain't gonna know if you're into that till you try it. Anyone who has never sucked a little dick doesn't really know which team they're batting for. How can you say you don't like watermelon if you never try it, for example?"

Chelsea snorted. "I think he has a point."

"Please don't encourage him. He only gets worse if you egg him on."

"Goes both ways, Miss Chelsea. If you'd like, I could arrange for an experimental partner. Little ditty sucking never killed anybody is all I'm saying. And I know a woman with a pair that would've gotten two orphanages through the Great Potato Famine of '42."

"Now you're just making up dates," I said.

"Like hell I am," Dick protested. "I was there."

"And if you try to get my—" I paused. I was about to say my girlfriend. What were we, even? Parents. That was a thought. "Please don't advise my employees to suck any "titties," I said after a brief pause.

Chelsea was smiling, but still fidgeting. Even Dick's ridiculous behavior wasn't quite enough to get her mind off me meeting her daughter, and I couldn't quite blame her.

"It's going to be fine," I said.

She surprised me by taking my hand and squeezing it on top of her lap. Neither of us seemed to be in a particular rush to break contact.

. . .

Luna rushed outside the third-floor apartment door when we reached the top of the stairs. She did a jumping hug toward Chelsea, who caught her and spun her into a tight embrace.

I looked at the little girl more critically than I had in the office a few days back. I scanned her for hints of me and was shocked to find them.

The dark hair with a tendency toward curling at the edges. The complexion that leaned a little toward pale. The eyes and eyebrows were like mirror images of my own.

I found myself grinning when she pulled away from Chelsea and noticed me.

"Mr. Grumpy!" Luna rushed over and hugged my leg.

I awkwardly patted her back. I knew Chelsea was watching me like a hawk, and I was honestly unsure of how to bring something like this up to a little kid.

Chelsea's brother was leaning in the doorway, watching us with folded arms. "Thanks for the huge check, Mr. Rose."

I nodded, following everyone into Chelsea's cramped apartment. I wasn't naïve, and I'd known it would be small. I just wasn't prepared to experience *how* small. The entire living space consisted of a room with a small kitchenette tucked off to one side. It was a glorified bedroom, and I found my blood boiling to think of the mother of my child and my daughter living in this kind of place.

Chelsea must've noticed something of my thoughts in my expression. "It's not much, but it's cozy."

"This is our bed," Luna said, jumping on the bed in the corner, which was just a mattress on the ground. It at least had a comfortable looking set of sheets and a comforter on it, along with a small stack of brightly colored kid blankets.

"It's nice."

Grant scoffed. "Speaking of how nice my sister's hovel is, when does that first paycheck from you guys roll in, anyway?"

"The end of this week. Why?"

Grant took a step closer. He was tall but built about as thickly as a young tree. "Because I still don't trust your greedy ass to pay her what you promised."

"Grant," Chelsea said quietly. "Could you give us some time alone, please?"

He snorted, shook his head, then headed to the hallway outside.

I jerked my thumb in the direction he'd left. "I don't think he's a huge fan."

Luna tilted her head at me. "He's a person, silly. If he was a huge fan, he'd have a plug coming out of his butt."

I let out a surprised laugh. Chelsea was smiling too.

"Your mom and I wanted to tell you something important, Luna…"

Luna waited patiently. I glanced toward Chelsea, who gave me a small nod of encouragement.

I got down on my knees so I'd be eye-to-eye with her. "There's a lot more your mom and I owe it to you to explain later, but I wanted you to know who I am. Luna, I'm your dad."

Her large eyes narrowed as she looked from me to Chelsea, then back to me. "But I asked mommy how babies are made. She said it's when a man and woman love each other very much. Then they press their bellies together and the boy shoots a baby from his belly button into—"

"That is not at all what I said," Chelsea said.

Luna smiled wide. "You two touched belly buttons, didn't you?"

"Yes," I said gravely. "Five years ago."

Luna burst out in giggles and Chelsea rolled her eyes. "Wait," she said, face suddenly going dead serious. "You're really my daddy?"

"Yeah." Why the hell did my throat feel so goddamn thick. And why was her apartment so stupidly dusty. "I'm your dad."

Luna launched forward, wrapping her small arms around my neck. "Hi," she whispered.

"Hi," I said, squeezing her tightly.

32

CHELSEA

Luna's spoon scraped the bottom of her cereal bowl as she tried to get the last drop of milk. "Can he spend the night tonight?"

"No," I said. I rubbed at my tired eyes. I'd barely slept last night with the way my thoughts were racing. "I don't know."

"Can I sleep over at his house?"

"No."

"But he's my daddy."

"He is, but it's more complicated than that."

Luna nodded wisely. "Because you two like touching each other's belly buttons?"

"No," I said. *Kind of.*

I spent the remainder of my time before I had to get Luna to school trying and failing to explain why adults didn't always say the things they felt, and how Damon and I were still trying to figure things out. In the end, Luna reverted to planning for the sleepover she thought was going to happen any day now.

I dropped her off at school and headed to work. I wasn't sure what to expect now that I'd unofficially been promoted by Damon during our "work trip." The funny part was that we'd only managed to sabotage a potential client acquisition and desperately complicate our personal lives over the weekend. It probably would've been better for everyone involved if we'd just stayed in New York.

I'd also spent all day yesterday waiting for someone to come explain my new duties, but nobody had spoken to me until I saw Damon head off toward the "interesting" thing Daria had mentioned. Needless to say, I hadn't accomplished anything that day.

I greeted the secretary, who always made one of two types of comments. She'd ask if I had a late night with a somewhat disturbing leer that told me she was hoping to live vicariously through me, or she'd make a sarcastic comment about how excited I must be to get to work. Either way, I smiled and appreciated the routine of it.

Little by little, I'd started to feel more at home here, even though my desk was practically designed to make me feel like an outsider in the spotlight.

But when I reached my floor, I couldn't find the awkwardly placed desk in the center of the room.

I thought about knocking on Damon's door, but for some reason, I was afraid to speak to him. He'd left off after he told Luna the truth, which had been followed by a long session of questions from her that had barely given me a chance to get a word in edgewise.

Now I had no real idea where we stood. I didn't know if he'd gone back to being pissed at me for keeping the secret. I didn't know if he was drafting wedding vows. I just didn't know.

All I *did* know is that my heart was still in a puddle from watching the two of them hug. It was breaking every time Luna asked about him with bright excitement in her eyes. It was everything I'd been afraid to hope for, and now I was too scared to make sure it was real. I worried I'd walk into his office and realize with one scowl that Damon was going to tear down the dream brick by brick.

So I found my way to the floor below ours where the HR department worked. After asking around for the appropriate person, I was sat down with a chipper young guy who couldn't have been much past twenty. He had bird-like features and a habit of humming nervously while he typed.

"Cross, you said, right?" he asked.

I nodded.

"Yep. Looks like Mr. Rose officially put in your promotion... Friday evening."

"As in last week before our business trip?"

"Yep, I guess? Congratulations, though, Miss Acquisitions Agent. Very fancy. You know, my brother's friend dated one of them. Said they make *crazy* money. I mean, so long as you aren't afraid of rubbing elbows with Mr. Rose. But who isn't?"

I smirked. "Yeah. He's a scary guy."

"I heard he fired an intern's entire family because she screwed up his coffee once."

"Her entire family worked here?"

The guy shrugged. "I didn't ask for details. They say if he finds out you are digging for or spreading gossip about him, he'll take you to the utilities closet and shove a mop handle so far up your ass that it comes out your nostrils."

I found myself smiling. Part of me almost wondered if Damon had gleefully spread those rumors himself. "Do 'they' realize the mop handle would have to reverse direction in your head to pull that off?"

The guy smiled a little uncomfortably. "Just what I heard. That's all. *Oh*, I also heard he once walked up to someone's desk and *spit* on their computer screen because they misplaced a comma in an email they sent him. Dude is a savage."

"Well, I'll be careful around him. I wouldn't want him shoving anything up my butt or spitting on me." I stopped myself from giggling like an immature schoolgirl. To tell the truth, I wasn't *entirely* sure either of those statements were true.

"Oh, by the way." The guy dug in his desk and pulled something out of a messy drawer. "I was going to mail this out later. Want to just take it now?"

He wiggled a manilla envelope toward me.

"Paycheck," he added with a wink.

I snatched it from his hands and hugged it to my chest. "I thought I wasn't supposed to get this until Friday?"

"Don't thank me, thank he who must not be named. And, uh, please don't tell him I said that. My name is Roy, by the way. But he sent a memo this morning telling me to pay you everything you were owed from your previous position immediately, now that you're working in acquisitions."

My eyes fell to his nametag, which said Peter. "Well, thanks, Roy. I had better get going."

"Hey, seriously don't tell him. Please. I was just kidding around. And I don't want him to take me to the closet."

I smiled. "Want an insider secret? Mr. Rose is all bark and no bite. You don't need to be so scared of him."

I WENT BACK TO MY FLOOR AND DECIDED TO STOP BEING SUCH A wuss. After all, I wasn't a wuss.

I was a stubborn, pain in the ass, never takes 'no' for an answer kind of girl. And in the right circumstances, one could even go as far as to call me a certifiable badass. *Okay, Chelsea. You're stretching the truth now.*

The point was I didn't plan to cower with my tail between my legs forever. Damon and I needed to have a conversation like two grown ass adults. That was all.

I knocked softly on Damon's office door. "Can I come in?" I asked.

There was a grunt from inside.

I walked in and saw Damon's computer monitor was covered in little pink scooters. "Do you think she'd like this one?"

"Who? Do you have a girlfriend I don't know about?"

"Luna."

I walked closer, suppressing a smile. Was he seriously planning to start showering her with gifts? I hoped he knew there wasn't enough room for much more than a few extra handfuls of air in my apartment. "She has been wanting one with just two wheels. She says those three wheeled ones are for 'kids.'"

"She *is* a kid. And wouldn't three wheels be safer?"

I patted his arm softly before I thought about what I was doing. "You have a lot to learn."

My hand on his arm seemed to wake both of us up to the reality of where we stood. He turned his attention from the computer to my hand. "We need to figure this out. *Us.*"

"Then I need to actually get to know you. More than just feelings and instincts. Or maybe real dates instead of business trips."

Damon nodded. "Tonight at seven. I'll pay your brother a thousand dollars to watch Luna for the night if that's what it takes."

"My brother would watch Luna for a ham sandwich, but something tells me a thousand dollars will do the trick, too."

"Good. Then it's a date. Also, your office is next door. Where Gary's used to be."

"What happened to Gary?"

"I promoted him so I could have the space for you."

"I can't decide if I should be disgusted or flattered."

"Get used to it. I want you now, Chelsea. Before, I wasn't sure what I wanted. Now I know exactly how this is going to play out. How it *needs* to play out."

God, Damon could be so intense. It was hard not to believe every single word that came out of his mouth when it came to what he was going to do. I wasn't sure the man was capable of failure. Except now he'd apparently decided failure would be if he didn't get me for himself. "How is that?"

"By doing whatever it takes. By not giving a shit that you work for me or that I'm your boss. You're going to be mine, and we're going to be a fucking family. Luna deserves that. *You* deserve it."

"Well, send Dick over at seven, then."

"You can have dick right now." He was completely straight faced, and I couldn't tell if he was joking until his lips curved up at the corners a few seconds later.

I shook my head. "It's unnerving when you try to be funny, you know."

"I'll work on it. Oh, and I don't care if we are fucking. If you want to keep your new position, I expect you to have signed your first athlete by the end of the week. If you have any questions about where to start, you can ask Judy. Don't ask David."

"Why not? I thought David was one of the top agents here."

"Because I don't want David staring at your breasts. Those are mine, too."

I felt a rush of heat spread in my stomach. Of course, there were the obvious workplace harassment arguments to be made. Except I didn't find myself wanting to make a single one of them. I wanted everything Damon seemed to want, and I had a feeling he knew it. But we both knew I couldn't just launch myself into a relationship blindly, not without being sure. Luna deserved that much from me.

"Got it. Show a little ass and David will be happy to help me with anything I need."

"Don't tempt me to use company time to fuck that naughty edge right out of your system."

I raised my eyebrows, then swallowed. I wished I had been clever enough to snap back with something witty, but all I could do was hold back the flood of deliciously sexy images bombarding my consciousness. Damon tearing that silky black shirt open and then spinning me around to bend over his desk.

His hands hungrily tearing at my clothes. The sensation of my arousal lubricating his thick length into me. My walls tight and—

"I'll be good," I said, cutting off my own desperate thoughts. This was bad. Self-control felt like a long-forgotten friend at the moment, and I knew my ability to resist jumping on Damon's lap was only held back by the faintest thread of resistance.

"And if I so much as think David or any other man in this office is interested in you, I'll abuse every ounce of my power to fire their ass straight out of your life."

I gulped. This was new, and I wished I could say I didn't like it in the dirtiest possible ways.

33

DAMON

The workday was winding down in slow, painfully drawn out minutes. It was just after four—only three hours until I'd have Chelsea to myself off company property—and I was leaned back in my office.

Chris was sitting across from me with a thoughtful look on his face. "You know, at first, I thought you were constipated. You've got this kind of pent up, frustrated look on your face. Then I saw Chelsea walk by just now. You perked up like a fucking dog at the sound of popping bacon." He smiled broadly. "Is my brother happy? Is he *actually* happy?"

I shook my head. "Happiness is an illusion. It's the pointless moment after you reach a goal and before you set the next. Spending your life chasing happiness would be as productive as spending your life trying to ejaculate."

Chris looked up at the ceiling, trying to process everything I'd just said. "Hm. Have you ever considered therapy?"

"I don't want to listen to people's problems. So, no."

He snorted. "No, I don't mean have you considered administering therapy to people. I mean, have you considered getting help. Because your brain is fucked up."

"If what I am is fucked up and what you are is normal, then I'm perfectly content."

"One of us has fun. The other sits in his office trying to reason with himself about why trying to be happy is pointless. Hmm. I wonder who has things more figured out."

I sighed. I never really confided in Chris. He came to me with his problems and I fixed them. It wasn't the other way around, even though I could tell he was trying to get me to open up and talk.

"Is there a reason you're in my office?" I asked.

"Yep." He was dressed in some kind of ridiculous tracksuit and a sleeveless shirt. I could at least appreciate that he was wearing gear from our biggest sponsor. They always liked it when the paparazzi got shots of our athletes in their gear. Free advertising.

"Hey!" Chris leaned in, snapping his fingers. "You're drifting on me. I can tell you're thinking about kicking puppies or doing your taxes or some shit. Focus."

"I am perfectly focused." Except Chelsea walked by again outside my door. Jane was leading her around, and Chelsea was trying to carry a giant stack of papers Jane appeared to have given her. Chelsea tried to scratch her nose with her elbow but dropped everything she was carrying. I saw her soundlessly apologizing, then laughing a little manically, then cleaning up with a sober expression while Jane glared down at her.

"Okay, now you're smiling," Chris said. He followed my eyes out the window of my office and clapped his hands, jabbing his finger at Chelsea. "Exactly! I fucking knew it. You're sticking your dick in that, and your dumbass doesn't understand the emotions it's causing you to feel."

"What? I was laughing because she did something stupid. I enjoy when people do stupid things and I get to watch."

"Yeah? Then maybe the secret to happiness would be locking you in a room full of mirrors."

Despite myself, I chuckled. Chris grinned back at me.

"See?" he said. "There's some human in there. It just takes a lot of fishing. Now, let me explain something to you about relationships. And no, you don't know shit about them. All you've ever done is find warm holes, and once or twice you brought the warm hole home from the store and rented it."

"That's disgusting."

"I know, you're a freak. But the point is that you actually like this one. I'm sure her pussy is great, but I think you like *her*. So if you want to make things work, you've got to stop being such a depressing grump. Smile a little. Make some jokes. Make her feel comfortable and wanted."

"This is your advice?"

Chris nodded. "Also go down on her. Don't be selfish in bed. Women love that shit."

I let out a long sigh. "Remind me why my brother—the same brother who moves through new women every week—is remotely qualified to give me relationship advice?"

"Because I don't just sleep with the women I'm with. Each relationship is a little, self-contained explosion of perfection. I wine them. I dine them. We bond. I get to know them, and they get to know me. I'm just addicted to the first part." He shrugged. "Things get boring after that."

"It still sounds like you're the worst person to give me advice." I trailed off as I was speaking. I saw David approach where Chelsea was picking up papers. His eyes were clearly on her ass as she bent down on her knees to scoop up the last few pages. He straightened his tie and took a step toward her.

I got up and moved for the door.

"Go get her, champ!" Chris urged. "Just hide that massive boner you're rocking so she doesn't think you're a creep."

I looked down, then groaned in annoyance.

Chris barked a laugh. "He always looks. This fucking guy."

Chris looked around the room, as if at an invisible audience that was eating up his dumb jokes.

"When I come back, I want you out of my office."

"Yeah, yeah." Chris waved me out the door.

David was helping Chelsea with the stack of papers when I stepped outside my office. "Did you wrap up the deal for that goalie, David?"

"Y-yes, sir. I mean, I still need him to sign some documents, but he always takes a while to get back to my emails."

"Then you didn't wrap it up. Why aren't you at your desk and on the phone?"

He made an apologetic face, handed Chelsea the papers he'd been carrying for her, and fast walked to his desk.

Chelsea gave me a dry look. "Really, Mr. Rose?"

Jane was waiting with folded arms.

"You can go back to work, too, Jane. I'll take over."

Her eyebrows shot up. All the superiority Jane had been wearing was gone in an instant. "Personally? You're going to train her?"

"Chelsea has shown me more potential in one week than anybody else here has shown me in their entire careers. Yes, I'm going to personally train her, and I'd fully expect you to be answering to her before long."

Chelsea was blushing, and Jane looked furious—but not stupid enough to talk back. She pressed her lips tightly together, then stormed off.

"You didn't have to do that," Chelsea said.

"Do what?"

"Lie for me. Chase off that David guy. Any of it, really."

"Yes, I do."

"Why?" she asked. There was a flash of sincere curiosity in her eyes. It was almost desperate. "Why me?"

"Because no matter how hard I tried to make everything else

matter... After you, nothing ever did. Even when I lied to myself and pretended otherwise. It was always you."

"Did you read that on a Hallmark card?"

"No. I'm trying to... Explain my feelings."

Chelsea wore a small smile as she stepped closer and adjusted my tie. "The way you're looking at me right now kinda says a lot."

"How am I looking at you?"

"Like you want to take me to the utility closet and put a broom up my ass. *Gently.*"

"What?"

She smirked. "Inside joke, sorry. But how do I know all this isn't just because you put a baby in me."

"For the record, you're still not off the hook for waiting five years to tell me about that."

Despite my teasing, I knew deep down she'd made the right choice. God only knew what I would've done five years ago—what I would've said. It had taken years of erosion for me to admit what I felt. I cared about Chelsea. Fuck, I probably loved her, and that was more ridiculous than it sounded. Just over a week ago, she hadn't been in my life for five years. And five years ago, she was a blip—just an explosion of perfect sex and the frustrating aftermath.

It had all been so brief, but somehow, she weighed on me still.

Chelsea peeked to see if anyone was looking, then gave me a little kiss on the cheek that was endearingly chaste. "Vulnerability is a good look on you, Mr. Rose."

My brother burst out of my office then. He let out a dramatic sigh. "I mean, come on. I was trying to be polite and let you guys have a little moment before I came out. But seriously, it has been like ten minutes and I've got to piss hard enough to take a urinal off the wall. Can I just—" Chris stuck his palm out, squeezing between us then half-jogged toward the bathroom.

Chelsea smiled after him, then turned back to me. "So, the

workday is over soon. Are you really going to personally train me, or was that all just to get a moment alone?"

"A little bit of both, but I meant what I said. I'll start officially teaching you tomorrow. Why don't you head home early and pick out something to wear for tonight? I expect to be salivating, and I know you won't disappoint me."

Chelsea worked her lips to the side and wiggled her eyebrows. "So I should wear my seared steak print dress, then?"

"I'm sure you'd look amazing in it, but I was thinking something tight and short. Something that won't put up much of a fight when I decide to tear it off of you."

She swallowed. "Not the meat dress, then. That one is a bitch to take off."

34

CHELSEA

I took one last look in the mirror, fiddled with my hair for the tenth time, then turned to Grant. "You're sure this is okay?"

He shrugged. "A thousand dollars to sleep on your couch and tell Luna there's no hungry hungry hippo under her bed? Yeah, I'll manage."

I grinned. "Can you believe she chose that to be afraid of, of all things?"

"Kind of. I'm pretty sure hippos kill more people than pretty much all the other so-called people killers. Sharks, bears—that kinda stuff."

"Okay, but we live in New York City. I'm pretty sure she's safe from hippos."

Luna had been drawing in the corner and decided to join the conversation. "I'm not a baby. I can hear you talking about me."

"Okay, Miss Big Kid. Answer me this. Our mattress is on the floor. How do you think a hippo could fit under there, anyway?"

"A trap door. *Duh.*"

Grant held up his palms in innocence. "I didn't teach her to say 'duh' so don't look at me."

"I learned it from the guy who sells hotdogs outside our apartment. *Duh*," she added.

I walked over to the mattress and lifted it, pointing to the floorboards beneath. "No trap doors. See?"

Luna folded her little arms. "There's never a trap door anywhere until somebody builds it."

I hung my head. "Okay. Good luck with her tonight, Grant."

He saluted. "Don't do anything I wouldn't do." He plopped his lanky frame down against the wall and stretched out his long legs. Sometimes I felt sad to see him this way because I could still remember so clearly how I thought of him when I was a little girl. He was my giant. My big brother who could do anything he wanted. Now, that version of him had withered away into something mild and sad. But with the money I was earning, and the new position Damon had given me, I'd help him.

I quietly promised myself that I'd use the opportunity I had to help turn his life back around. I'd get him his own place and see him happy again.

Outside, I was surprised to find Damon waiting for me with a bouquet of something green and strong-smelling. I squinted at it but didn't see any flowers or recognize it. "Are these weeds?" I asked.

He deflated a little. "I thought flowers would be too cliché. They're also pointless. So I brought you something practical. They're herbs. I picked them from an organic rooftop garden. It's dill, rosemary, and thyme. I thought you could make some roast potatoes with them or something."

I laughed, taking the bundle of wild greenery and sniffing. "That's actually sweet, even if it's a little weird. So... Should I go put these in water?"

Damon nodded.

Grant gave me a baffled look when I set all the herbs down on the counter. "I'll explain later," I said, giving Luna a quick kiss and hug before heading back downstairs to Damon.

He was dressed in a suit and tie that he wore so comfortably I wasn't sure he ever took them off. The tie tonight was a navy blue that made his eyes look startlingly bright.

"I see you decided against the steak dress," he noted as he stuck his elbow out for me.

"Are we walking to our date?" I hooked my arm in his with a little smile. "This is very formal."

"Dick got lost on the way here. He's parked like two blocks away. I had to tell him to stop trying to get closer because he kept getting farther every time I tried to guide him."

I chuckled. "How does he get lost? It's just a bunch of squares. He's also been here before."

"Dick is a shit driver. He bangs up his car almost every week, and I'm starting to suspect he even ran someone over once."

We joined the late evening crowd of people traveling the sidewalks, heading North at an easy pace. "I'm starting to think you're nowhere near as hard as you led people into believing."

"Only when it comes to certain people. I'm just very particular."

"So I met your particular criteria? Is that it?"

"Something like that. Yes."

We walked in silence for a while, then. It was just his strong arm hooked with mine and his steady footsteps. There was the occasional honk of a car and the wet sound of tires rolling through streets still wet from the evening's rain.

It was a beautiful night, and I felt completely alive next to him.

Except I couldn't relax into the moment and this idea. I couldn't just accept that we'd arrived, and everything was going to be okay, because I still didn't feel like the chapter on this Trish woman was closed. I didn't know why I felt that way, but she loomed in my chest like a blockage—something hard and unforgiving standing between us and where I wanted to be. I knew I was getting close to a solution with her, but I still couldn't completely shake the feeling of dread.

Maybe it was just that I didn't trust her not to show up with her arms outstretched and a crazy glint in her eyes—to say *no, you shall not pass*! It was ridiculous but knowing so didn't help me shake the feeling.

We reached Dick's car after a pleasant walk and found him doing a crossword puzzle on the steering wheel. He grinned wide at us, showing off a squared off gap from where he'd lost a tooth. "There's the lovebirds."

Damon played the gentleman and opened the door for me. Except when he put his hand on my lower back to guide me into the seat, I noticed he managed to make it feel far, far more sexual than the simple touch should've.

I sat there trying to calm down the explosion of warmth between my legs as he walked around the back of the car to get in. Damon's touch triggered a chemical reaction in me. He made me realize there were three states of consciousness—not two. Asleep, awake, and those moments when our skin was pressed together. The promise of what was to come from his fingertips was an electric shock to my system that vaulted me into an absolute height of awareness.

Damon stole a glance when he sat down, then scooted close enough for our legs to press together. I'd imagined a night of deep conversations. Of revealed vulnerability and open hearts. Now all I could think about was the hardness between his legs and how full I'd feel when he gave it to me tonight.

God. How was I supposed to function around this man?

Dick looked up at us through his rearview, tapping his ear. "Now I can turn my hearing aides off if you two youngsters want to have a little privacy back there."

"How young do you think we are, exactly, Dick?"

"When you get to my age, young is anyone you don't check the obituaries for as a daily habit."

"Or people who don't still read the newspaper," I suggested.

"Young people also still have the energy to be sassy. That's one of the first things that goes. Sassiness. Well, that and not looking like a melted candle when I strip down for the shower."

Damon shot me a half smile. "Thanks for the imagery, Richard."

Dick drove for what felt like an hour before we arrived. I passed the time by playing a red-hot game of eye fucking with Damon. I'd never been the type to engage in ocular relations in the backseat of a car, especially one piloted by a grumpy old Dick. But Damon brought out my naughty side, and I was uncomfortably wet by the time we arrived.

It was going to be a long, excruciatingly enjoyable night, and it was just getting started.

"Where are we, exactly?"

Damon got me out of the car—still playing the gentleman, apparently. "We're at your first lesson as an acquisitions agent. If you want to acquire someone, you start by wowing them."

I looked around. To tell the truth, I couldn't have said if we'd driven North, South, or burrowed our way out of the city. We were parked in some sort of grassy, well-lit garden paradise. The road leading up to the hedges was made of decorative pavers and lit by ornate lamp posts. It looked nothing like downtown or anything near it, and it was deafeningly quiet except for a faint rustling of leaves.

"I feel like someone with a British accent is going to emerge from the hedges at any minute. What the hell is this place?" I asked.

Damon gestured wide to the path we'd driven up, where Dick was now slowly reversing the car to leave us by ourselves. "This is a road. They've been used for centuries to—"

"Damon," I warned.

He took a step backward, heading closer to the hedges that wound out of sight. "Do you want to learn or not?"

"I thought this was a date," I said, having to raise my voice as he headed up the path.

"Multitasking. That's lesson two," Damon called over his shoulder.

I rolled my eyes but jogged to catch up with him.

I had time to take in more of my surroundings. Tall trees towered above us and seemed to catch every hint of the breeze, sending down peaceful whispers to my ears. I ran my hand along the hedges, which were trimmed perfectly flush with the path like leafy green walls.

All I could see was Damon walking ahead of me, occasionally glancing back with an uncharacteristic lightness and excitement in his eyes. I could see the trees and the hedges—the path below us.

I realized how much trust I was placing in him in this moment. For all I knew, we were seconds from the part where he reveals this has all been a ruse. He pulls out the knife, laughs, and plunges it home as I scream in my native tongue—idiot—for not seeing it coming.

Except I didn't really believe that. I did trust Damon. I trusted him more because he'd started this whole thing out by trying to push me away.

For some reason, that made me trust him so much more. Maybe it was because I'd had the chance to watch him try and fail to stop himself from falling for me.

We finally exited the footpath through the gardens, and I got a glimpse of what we'd been heading toward. There was a colonial style mansion sitting atop a gently rolling grass hill. Windswept oaks and endless manicured lawns surrounded the property. Everything was tastefully lit, including a tennis court that was hardly visible through tall, wall-like hedges.

I arched an eyebrow. "Did you ask me to dress up to challenge me to a tennis match? Were you hoping I couldn't still whip your ass in heels?"

Damon shook his head, pointing. "I thought it might be a treat for a tennis enthusiast to watch two of the best up close."

I frowned, then heard the telltale pop of a ball being served. Years and years on the court had trained me to judge the speed of a hit from the sound alone, and I knew immediately there was a professional in there. "Who is that?"

"Trevor Castle."

I paused. "The same Trevor Castle who you nearly killed in Savannah?"

Damon gestured for me to follow him toward the courts. "Lesson three. There's no such thing as a burned bridge if you bring your 'A' game to the negotiation table."

"What'd you offer him, your left nut?"

"Why would he want that?"

I chuckled. "I keep forgetting you have the sense of humor of a wet rock."

"Ah. So the wet ones aren't as funny as the dry ones?"

I grinned. Damon smirked back.

Inside the court, Trevor was rallying against Edgar Warren, another top ten player. I felt a little silly walking toward the cozy little lounge chairs for spectators. Trevor and Edgar's coaches were wandering around behind the baseline, occasionally feeding balls in for the men to rally with. It felt like I should've been wearing a skort and carrying my bag to be here. My heels and short dress felt completely out of place, but I was willing to deal with it if it meant watching this up close.

Trevor noticed us. "Ready for the match?" he called to Edgar.

Edgar gave a thumbs up.

For the next hour, we sat in the perfect evening air watching a private showing of amazing tennis. Neither player held back, and I even forget I was sitting next to Damon a time or two.

I did keep catching him stealing glances my way. I grinned,

then bumped my knee into his. "Pretty proud of yourself for this one, aren't you?"

"That depends."

"On?"

Trevor swore under his breath and spiked a ball into the net in front of us, drawing a laugh from Edgar.

"It depends on whether this worked."

"Well," I said, tilting my head toward him. "I need to know what your goal was before I can say if it worked."

Damon, paying no mind to anyone else, slid a hand up my knee to my inner thigh. My insides practically exploded with need. I pressed my thighs together, putting my hand on his and checking to see if anyone had seen. "Damon!" I whispered.

He didn't take his eyes from my legs for a few long, heart-pounding moments. When he looked up, I thought he was about to tear my clothes off right there. "I'm tired of waiting."

"It has barely been twenty-four hours. How impatient are you?" I asked.

"For you? About as patient as my brother at a Broadway play."

"Chris isn't a fan of Broadway?" I asked. I was stalling. A very distinct part of me still wanted to absorb every second of tennis that was playing out in front of me. Another part of me wanted to buy time—to *think*. But thinking when his hand was between my legs and his eyes were driving straight through my soul was a little easier said than done.

"Chris once asked if we could bribe the director to fast forward to the third act."

"So what you're saying is you want to *bone* me. Badly."

"Those aren't the words I'd use."

"Which words would you use?" I asked. God, I felt so embarrassingly turned on. I could've almost—*almost*—been convinced to try to kiss him, just because I was craving more of his touch that badly. Except I'd been permanently scarred with my middle school boyfriend in seventh grade. He'd held my hand in the hallway and the dean had yanked our hands apart before yelling, "P.D.A.!" Of course, everyone laughed their asses off at us, and I swore on everything holy that I'd never engage in a public display of affection again.

"Which words…" Damon's eyes looked heavy. Hungry. They skidded across my features and his full lips parted. "I'd tell you that I want to fuck you until you feel me all day tomorrow. I'd say I want to mark you. I want to kiss your neck until it bruises so nobody else has to wonder if you're taken. And I want to taste you again. Every fucking inch."

"I see," I said, gulping. "I guess that's a little more descriptive than saying you want to bone me."

35

DAMON

Chelsea personally thanked the tennis players when they'd finished their match. I had to grit my teeth when she shook Trevor Castle's hand. I could just imagine how he still wanted a shot with her, and it made me want to slam him up against another wall.

It was stupid, I knew. A deep, uncontrollable protectiveness had been building inside me for Chelsea. I had five years to make up for. Five years that she'd been struggling to work multiple jobs. Five years of sacrifices to protect her daughter. *Our* daughter.

I owed her the world, and I was only just beginning to feel it sink in.

Still, I behaved. I didn't say a word as she had a quick and casual conversation with the players and their coaches.

Chelsea followed me out of the tennis courts when they were done.

Trish Jameson was waiting outside the court with Tia Klein when we emerged. Both women looked smug.

I put one hand in front of Chelsea, almost as if I expected

them to try to pounce on her. "Who told you we were here?" I demanded.

Tia raised her hand and eyebrows. "Turns out your staff is extremely horny and open to persuasion. I practically just had to breathe on your security guard to get access to your agenda."

"Do I want to know why either of you are here?"

"Probably not," Trish said. "But Tia is going to be working with me from now on. I figured I'd have the same conversation with Trevor once we're done here, too."

I clenched my teeth. My brother's situation had been deteriorating with his team. In other words, Rose Athletic needed faces like Tia Klein and Trevor Castle. I'd be lying if I said losing both wouldn't be a serious blow. "What's this really about, Trish?"

She smirked. "The same thing it has always been about. You don't deserve the things you have. I do. So I'll take them, and I'll keep taking them until I'm satisfied."

I shook my head. Before I could speak, Chelsea pushed forward.

"We'd like to see you try, bitch."

Easy there, Killer. "How about this," I suggested. "You keep trying to do whatever is you're doing, and we'll continue not giving a shit. Sound fair?"

Trish scoffed. "You can pretend all you want, Damon. I know this is hurting your bank account."

"My bank account will survive. Thanks for the concern. And you, Tia. You're sure you want to team up with her? She's more worried about screwing me over than how this turns out for you."

Tia shrugged. "Maybe next time you'll be a little smarter when one of your athletes needs a little special attention."

I sighed. So it was about that? I knew I could go to Trevor and try to prepare him for whatever bullshit Trish and Tia were about to throw his way. Instead, I took Chelsea's hand and led her toward the large house. I'd planned a date, and I didn't intend for Trish or Tia to ruin that.

Chelsea looked back as I pulled her away. "That's all? Aren't we going to throw down or something?"

"No. They're not worth it."

"Is she right, though? Can you afford to lose both Tia and Trevor?"

"So long as Chris keeps his head out of his ass? Yes."

We headed toward the large house in silence until Chelsea finally spoke. "It's going to be hard to top that," she said. "I mean, the surprise appearance from the two wicked bitches of the west was a twist I didn't see coming. So far, we've had sports and drama. What else do you have planned to round out the evening, Mr. Rose?"

I chuckled. She had such a sexy way of saying 'Mr. Rose,' and I was almost certain she knew it. "Winning clients is about winning confidence. Start with the heavy guns. It loosens them up and they'll be more open to persuasion."

She gave me a funny look. "And what do you do if the agent trying to persuade you is trying to keep you at arm's length?"

I stopped. We were just outside the front porch of the mansion with giant oak double doors to our side. "Arm's length?" I wrapped my hand around her waist and pulled her close to me. "If you mean like this..."

"No," she said, pulling back. "I mean how I feel like I need to know the whole story with this Trish woman. I feel like there's more than you're letting on. And I mean, yeah. I'm attracted to you. Yeah, you gave me an awesome job. Yeah, I appreciate everything. But *you*. I need to know the real you."

I took a deep breath. "Okay. What do you want to know?"

"I want to know what happened with you two."

"It was complicated."

"That's not good enough. I know she screwed you over. She stole your clients. Broke your heart, probably. But I still feel like there's something you're not telling me, and there can't be any more secrets."

I walked to a swinging bench and sat down. Chelsea moved beside me, sitting cross legged and turning so she could face me. I heard the laughter of the tennis players and their coaches as they were apparently being charmed by Trish in the distance.

I'd hoped to skip this part. Maybe forever. But Chelsea was right. We couldn't make a functional relationship on the fact that we liked to sleep together. For me, I didn't really need to know anything else about her. I knew there were dark corners I'd discover someday—little secrets and fun facts. But I also knew how I felt when I was around her and how different it was than being around anyone else.

"Trish and I weren't just together. We actually got married. Five years ago. It was the kind where we went to the altar in plain clothes and signed some papers afterwards. I'd been trying to fill a void for so long that she came along and I guess—" I trailed off, shaking my head. "I guess I thought love was the sort of thing you had to build from scratch, like a business."

"You *married* her? Wait, you said this was five years ago. How long after we…"

"A month, maybe two."

Chelsea paused. "What void were you trying to fill, exactly?"

"The one that opened up after you walked out of my life."

It was true, too. I'd been too stupid to see it at the time, but it was so true it stung. It had always been Chelsea, and I'd burned myself a hundred times trying to find a way to replace the way she'd made me feel.

"You hated me," she said.

"No. I wanted to hate you. I didn't want to need anyone or anything. Then you fucked that up, didn't you?"

Chelsea looked up in thought. "I guess while we're confessing, I should confess that I thought you were a grumpy, unforgivable asshole from the moment I met you. And I wanted to die when I realized I was going to apply to work for you. And I may have wished once or twice that a lightning bolt would strike you dead while you were on the toilet."

I frowned. "These aren't the kinds of confessions I was hoping for."

"But," Chelsea said, holding up her index finger. "I also used to tease the boys I liked in school. And I maintained that cooties should've been classified as a deadly virus by the CDC until late middle school. So I guess what I'm saying is that you can't always trust what I say or do when it comes to my feelings."

"What can I trust, then?"

She gnawed on the inside of her lip, staring down at her hands in her lap. "The fact that I'm here. With you. That my heart is pounding, and my body feels alive. I want this, Damon. Whatever it is. I want it."

I cupped her cheek, pulling her toward me for a kiss.

I wasn't the sentimental type, but I discreetly made sure I remembered every fucking sensation I was feeling. I memorized the soft warmth of her cheek against my palm. I focused on the velvety touch of her wet lips and the heat of her tongue. I listened to the insects chittering and the leaves of the trees rustling over our heads. And I thought about how inside—deep inside my chest—there was a void that I'd never quite managed to plug up. Except right now, with my hands on Chelsea, I couldn't find it. I couldn't even find a trace.

She pulled back after a few minutes of kissing with a small smile. "This was your plan all along, wasn't it? I thought you were going to do something cliché like a personal chef making us dinner by candlelight."

At that moment, the front door slowly opened. A nervous looking man in a chef's hat stuck his head out, and I was glad Chelsea's back was to him.

He opened his mouth to speak, but I discreetly waved my hand for him to go back inside.

"You've got to give me more credit than that," I said.

"From now on, I will." She hugged herself tightly against my chest.

36

CHELSEA

Damon was adorably embarrassed when we eventually went inside the house. He mumbled something about dinner, which was exactly as cliché as I'd teased him about.

He'd apparently arranged for a meal to be cooked and served in the decadent dining hall of the house. The whole building screamed colonial 1800s, big dresses, and coattails. It was charming, and I found myself swiveling my head when we sat down to admire the paintings and ornate wood paneling covering the walls. "This place is beautiful."

"I'm glad you like it."

Damon unfolded his napkin and set it in his lap. "In my defense, there are no candles."

I yanked the pull cord on the lamp between us, grinning. "A lamp-lit dinner. It's like you're deliberately trying not to be cliché now."

A waiter brought our plates and left the room.

I looked at Damon, trying not to laugh. "I feel like you're trying to apologize for something with all of this."

"Maybe I am."

"I feel like the one who has been on thin ice. I kept Luna a secret from you."

"And I made you think you needed to."

I hadn't touched my food, but I looked down at it, unsure what to say.

"Chelsea." Damon reached across the table and took my hand. "I don't want to downplay the importance of this conversation. But that steak in front of you is imported Kobe beef. The chef cooked it to the exact temperature where the fat will melt in your mouth. If we sit here and talk too long, it'll get cold."

I snorted. "Unbelievable."

He forked a piece of meat from my plate and held it toward my mouth. "It will be, if you stop talking long enough to try it."

Grinning, I took a bite. As promised, it was delicious. I wiped the corner of my mouth, savoring the buttery aftertaste. "I didn't realize you were in such a hurry to put your meat in my mouth tonight."

Damon choked on his water, then set it down, composing himself. "If my meat was in your mouth, you wouldn't be able to talk around it."

I wiggled my eyebrows. "That sounds like the sort of challenge meant to bait me into giving you a blowjob."

"I'm not too proud to resort to tricks."

∽

When we finished dinner, Damon took me upstairs. I noticed the wait staff and chef appeared to have left once our food was served, and as far as I could tell, we were alone in the huge building.

"What comes next?" I asked.

"If everything goes according to plan, you will."

Damon, the man who apparently had all the jokes now, scooped me up and carried me into a bedroom with a four-poster bed and silk drapes. I didn't have time to notice anything else before I was tossed onto the cloud-like mattress. I laughed up at him. "What if I refuse you, *boss?*"

"Then I'm going to have an unfortunate case of blue balls tomorrow."

"Hmm. That *would* be a shame. Especially since you passed up on Tia Klein earlier. I'm sure she would've loved to help you with that."

"I'd pass up a thousand Tia Klein's for a shot with you. Easily."

"Nine hundred and ninety-nine to go. I guess those balls are going to be blue for a while, aren't they?"

Damon made a low sound in his throat and pulled me toward him by the ankle. He was standing at the edge of the bed and had taken his tie off at some point. I sat up, gripping the front of his shirt.

"I see you're playing make believe," Damon said. He traced a goosebump inducing path down my cheek. "Pretending you aren't soaking wet for me. Pretending you wouldn't do every little thing I say. Pretending you aren't absolutely starving to have my cock buried inside you."

"I don't know if it'd do much good to bury it in me. I was thinking more about penetration."

Damon pushed me down by the chest, reaching for his buttons. "You're funny now, but that only makes it more satisfying to fuck the humor right out of you."

"I don't think it works that way."

He was on the bed now, shirtless and coming toward me. The muscles on his arms flexed with each movement, veins straining against his smooth skin.

"I want to taste you." Damon pushed up my dress, revealing the panties I'd worn specifically for him. I hoped he thought they were sexy. They had little bits of pink lace framing the black—

There was a sudden jerking motion and a ripping sound.

Damon was holding my torn panties in a victorious fist, his eyes hungry on my bare pussy. "Did you really just—"

His head was between my legs, and it felt like my body was pinned to the bed. My eyelids fluttered as his tongue drove into me and his hands explored me, reaching and groping like he could barely control himself.

Okay. Admittedly, it *was* harder to think in my natural sarcastic state of mind. In fact, it was hard to think. Period.

I took a handful of his hair, licking my lips as he licked mine. I grinned at my stupid twist on words just before he slid two fingers into me while his tongue worked.

My legs tried to close in reflexively, but he used his other hand to pry them forcefully open, which let him push his fingers even deeper.

I bucked against him, gasping.

"Fuck my hand," he rasped.

I obeyed, shamelessly gripping his arm for leverage as I moved myself against his hand.

When I thought another few seconds would have my gasps of pleasure filling the empty mansion, he pulled his fingers from me. He brought them to my mouth with hungry eyes. "Clean these off."

I was gasping and my body already felt light and fuzzy, but I still couldn't resist messing with him. "Have any baby wipes? Or maybe a pine scented cleaner?"

Damon used his thumb to part my lips with one hand and then brought his fingertips to my mouth with the other. "Clean them."

I bit my lip, then took his fingers in my mouth and sucked them. I could taste myself on him, and while it wasn't exactly something I'd order at my favorite restaurant, I had to admit it was exactly the kind of dirty to make my belly throb for him.

Damon did that to me. He made me feel out of control.

He made me hungry down to my core.

He made me want his fullness—the sensation of my walls gripping him tight.

I didn't have to wait long to get what I wanted.

Damon groaned as he watched me clean his fingers, then he pulled down his pants and positioned himself between my legs as I lay on my back.

"I want to have you bare. No condom."

"Is that smart?" *No, Chelsea. It is not. The man's sperm is basically an Olympic caliber swimming team a few million strong. You let those puppies anywhere near you, and you'll be pregnant.*

"I'll pull out. I need to feel you. All of you."

"If you knock me up, I will knock you out."

Damon flashed a half smile. "Terrifying."

The truth was I couldn't care. My mind was all fuzzy white light and *need*. It overwhelmed everything else. I wanted to feel him bare inside me, too.

He gripped my thighs and pulled me closer to him, then eased himself inside me.

I gasped, pulling him down by the neck to kiss him. Damon kissed me back. It wasn't like the other times we'd slept together.

His kisses were soft. Tender. *Loving.*

We found a rhythm together, moving in silence as our lips pressed together and our tongues met. I didn't know if it was only moments or several minutes, but when my orgasm came, it shook through my whole body. I felt myself tighten around his length inside me. Damon had been breathing heavily, and he moved to his knees, pulling himself free just before he came across my stomach.

I'd never been particularly drawn to the idea of getting covered in a man's come, but with Damon, I liked it. I liked being marked by him. Claimed, in some way.

"Question," I said once I caught my breath. "How do you plan to clean *me* up?"

Damon's deep chuckle shook through the mattress. "No way in hell."

37

DAMON

I'd always been someone who appreciated patterns. Routines. A rhythm.

It wasn't long before Chelsea and I found ours.

I'd spend time at her new place—the one she funded with her first paycheck. It was a two bedroom, which gave Luna some space to actually play and both of them to breathe. I also gradually built up an assortment of toys at my own apartment to make Luna's time fun when they came to visit.

Grant would happily take my checks and watch Luna when we wanted a date night, and between time with Luna, dates, and work, we were hardly ever apart. I still never seemed able to get enough of her, though. I took her in my office once and another time in the parking garage after hours.

I couldn't get enough of her.

Her scent.

Her moans.

The little smile and sigh she always let out after she came on my cock or my mouth or my fingers.

At work, we brainstormed how to solve our most pressing problems.

We were seated in the conference room with a handful of my senior administrative staff. Chelsea had only been in her role as an acquisitions agent for two weeks and a member of Rose Athletic for a total of three weeks, but she had exactly the kind of mind for the work. I had to give credit to my staff for taking her seriously, too.

It would've been easy for them to write her off as a pretty face who only was where she was because she was sleeping with me—a fact we tried and failed to hide from my staff. Ironically, the information I'd expected to undermine their respect for me had seemed to humanize me in some ways. The usual tension and thickness of atmosphere at Rose Athletic was noticeably diminished, and I couldn't say I minded.

"We'll be down forty percent next quarter. Tia Klein and Trevor Castle leaving in the same week shook confidence," Emma explained. She was one of my long-time admins—a woman in her sixties with a no bullshit attitude.

Chelsea set down the pad she'd been jotting notes on. "The problem isn't the money from Tia and Trevor's contracts, exactly. People's confidence is shaken in Rose."

Emma shrugged. "Okay. But what does that do for us? How do we use that?"

Chelsea chewed the tip of her pen. "Well, it's a branding issue. Rose was like the elite force in athletic representation. We have the best of the best with Chris Rose, and that spoke for itself. If you wanted to be like Chris Rose, you joined Rose. But when we brought attention with Tia and Trevor, we opened ourselves up to this. Now it looks like Chris is just Damon's brother, which undermines trust in our abilities."

"Okay," Emma said. "So, we do what, though?"

"Change the brand," Chelsea said. She shot me a look. I didn't understand what she seemed to be silently asking me permission for at first. She scribbled something on her pad, then held it up so only I could see.

Make your real dream public?

I sat back in my chair, frowning. I'd obviously opened up to Chelsea about what really drove me. I'd even gone into quite a bit of detail with her. She knew how badly I wanted to help young athletes avoid getting taken advantage of. But the idea of showing the world that felt terrifying. It seemed like turning my back to a crowd of people with knives in their hands.

But when I saw the earnest hope in Chelsea's eyes, I wanted to trust her. I nodded my head.

She smiled at me, then squeezed my leg under the table in a silent "thank you."

For the next ten minutes, she ran the room through a plan so detailed I was almost positive she hadn't thought about it on the spot. Basically, she wanted to take my secret charity cases I did on the side and turn them into the main purpose of Rose Athletic. Take the teams we used to spot talent and set up elaborate events to lure in new clients and use them to find athletes who needed our help.

The cornerstone of her plan was to add a branch of our business designed to be a school for upcoming athletes. We'd have a training program designed to teach them what to look for and how to avoid falling into the same traps so many athletes did. Financial training, tax courses, and everything else they'd need.

When she was finished, the room was silent for several long seconds.

"I love it," I said, breaking the quiet.

An explosion of voices followed as my staff worked out the details and ran over her ideas. Within an hour, we'd settled on something close to a final plan, and I couldn't have been more fucking proud of Chelsea.

38

CHELSEA

Luna and I met Damon for lunch a couple weeks after we initiated the plan to transform Rose Athletic. The weather was cool and sunny, so we took a seat outside on the patio by the street. Luna had on her heart shaped sunglasses and a shirt that read: "I'd care if I could."

She sipped her smoothie while we waited for Damon to arrive.

"What's daddy's favorite color?" She asked.

"Probably black," I said.

Luna frowned. "No. I think Daddy likes orange."

"Not many people pick orange as a favorite color."

"Orange is the tastiest color."

I laughed. "If you could only eat one color for the rest of your life, it'd really be orange? You wouldn't be able to eat strawberries or bananas. You love those."

Luna pursed her lips. "French fries are orange. Halloween donuts are orange. Chicken nuggets..." She scrunched her little face up as she tried to think of more examples.

"You might actually have a point. Maybe orange would be the way to go."

Damon surprised me from behind with a tight hug. He kissed my neck, then stole a kiss on my lips too that wasn't entirely appropriate for public places.

"You kiss like people in movies," Luna noted.

Damon took a chair beside us. "Because people in movies kiss the best."

"What's your favorite color, Daddy?"

"Orange," Damon said without a moment's pause.

Luna gave me the most triumphant smile imaginable, and I couldn't help laughing.

"What?" Damon asked. "It's the tastiest color," he said, winking at me.

Oh, I thought. Luna already had this conversation with him. It was a set up. Sly little turd.

I noticed someone walking by our table had stopped before I saw who it was. When I looked up, I felt a jolt of disgust to see Trish Jameson standing there. She didn't quite have the same cocky, superior air about her that she usually had.

"Really, Damon?" she asked.

Damon calmly took off his sunglasses and looked up at her. "Is there something you needed, Trish?"

"To tell you that you're making a big mistake. You realize the reason I was able to steal clients from under your nose was because this little dream of yours is so ridiculous, right? It scares away athletes. It makes you look soft, and the best don't want to be represented by someone soft."

"Great," Damon said. "Because our new business model doesn't rely on getting the best. I can feel good about what I'm doing, and coincidentally, I also get to know you don't have anything to hang over my head."

A little tick of rage flashed across her features. In that moment, I suspected keeping Damon under her designer heel had meant far more to Trish than I'd even imagined. "You're making a mistake."

"Speaking of mistakes," Damon said slowly.

I felt goosebumps spread across my body in preparation. He and I had been working on something in secret for the past couple weeks, and I knew he was about to drop it on Trish's head like a pile of rotten eggs. *I couldn't wait.*

"We hired a few accountants to look into your agency. A few little red flags popped up for me over the years, but I never had time to really look into them. The numbers you liked to brag to me about, the deals your clients had, their publicly listed earnings. There were some discrepancies. But once you took Tia and Trevor off my hands, I had enough time to really look into it."

Trish's face was getting progressively redder by the minute.

"I wonder what your athletes would say if they knew you've been embezzling money from them? If they knew you are skimming percentages off their earnings in every single way you possibly can?"

"Who did you talk to?" Trish demanded.

Damon laughed. "Nobody, yet. We wanted you to know what we know—to know we have all the proof we need to bring your shit-caked empire down brick by brick. And when we feel like it, that's exactly what we'll do."

"You're wrong," Trish said. She waved her finger between us —even at Luna, who pretended she was trying to bite at it. "You're *so* wrong."

With that, she stormed off as she jabbed her long nails at her phone screen.

"What do you think she'll do?" I asked.

"I'm not sure," Damon said. "But I think she bought it."

"What did she buy?" Luna asked.

"We played a little bit of a trick on her. But she was a mean woman, and sometimes mean people need to learn lessons."

Luna nodded wisely. "Jimmy at Pre-K bites people. We should get a tiger to bite him."

"Uh, not exactly like that," I said.

The truth was, Damon and I had investigated Trish like we said. Except our digging hadn't turned up any hard evidence. All we had were clues and hints, but nothing concrete enough to do anything with. We ultimately decided to bluff and see if we could force her to panic. Our accountants were watching every angle they could of her finances, and the way she reacted to our accusation might end up bringing the truth to light.

Whatever happened, it had been almost entirely worth it to see the look of pure fear in her eyes.

"No," Luna said quietly. "A hippo." She whispered the word like it held some sort of mystical power. "Jimmy needs to get bit by a hippo."

If the hippo was willing to bite Trish while he was at it—maybe Tia and Trevor, too—I'd personally go pay him for his services.

39

DAMON

Luna was riding the pink scooter I'd bought her around my apartment. In just a few days, she'd mastered all sorts of dangerous maneuvers that had Chelsea constantly reminding her to be careful. At the moment, she seemed to be trying to learn to drift around the corner from the dining room to the library.

My laptop screen was open to a story about Trish Jameson and the fallout when her embezzling scheme was uncovered.

"Read it again," Chelsea said. She leaned back in her chair to sip her morning coffee with a wide smile. "Just one more time, please."

I smirked, then cleared my throat. There was an image of Trish shielding her eyes as she hurried out of her former offices while being swarmed by reporters at the top of the article. "Trish Jameson, a leading agent in the world of professional sports, was charged with felony embezzlement this week as evidence of her wrongdoings mounted. Jameson's clients have fled the agency in droves, including big names and recent signees Tia Klein and Trevor Castle.

"Details are still to come, but for now, it appears that Trish Jameson's time as one of the top agents in the country are certainly over. In the coming months, we'll know if her actions will land her a lengthy prison sentence, fines, or both."

The article continued to go into detail about some of the allegations, but the part Chelsea wanted was the top.

"It feels so good," she said. "Am I a bitch for relishing in the idea of her getting her ass handed to her?"

"No," I said. "You also wouldn't be a bitch if you were happy to learn that Tia and Trevor are having trouble finding an agent after those anonymous stories about sexual harassment leaked."

Chelsea grinned into her cup. "I still have no idea how those got out."

IT HAD BEEN OVER A MONTH SINCE CHELSEA CAME TO WORK FOR ME at Rose Athletics. The weather was turning crisp more often, and Luna's giggles and growls were starting to become part of the soundtrack of my evenings and mornings.

It felt different, and it felt good.

So fucking good.

It was late and Chelsea had joined me on the balcony of my apartment for a glass of wine. She wore a thin floral print dress that, like everything else she ever put on, seemed too sexy to be fair. I hooked my hand around her waist when she got up to look over the balcony and pulled her into my lap.

I kissed her neck, smelling the scent of her shampoo and that intoxicating, indefinable aroma her skin always had. She let out a little moan, leaning into me and running her hand through my hair.

"I think I love you." I hadn't planned to say the words. I hadn't even dwelled on the fact that I hadn't told her I loved her before. But the moment I heard it aloud, I felt each syllable like it was sinking deep into my chest.

She turned her head, eyes searching mine. "You'd better

know if you're going to start throwing around statements like that."

I grinned. "I do. I love you, because if I didn't, there's no way I would be able to put up with you."

She swatted at me but closed her eyes and leaned into my shoulder. "Yeah, well, the feeling's mutual."

"You'd better say it," I warned. I stood, picking her up with me. "It's a long way down."

Chelsea widened her eyes, laughing. "You absolutely would not throw me to my death. It won't count if I'm only saying I love you to save my life."

"Say it," I warned, inching closer to the edge.

In a robotic voice, Chelsea said, "I. Love. You."

She tickled my armpits, which was a weakness she'd unfortunately discovered, and wormed her way out of my grasp. She stopped at the sliding door and gave me a taunting smile. "There's something I want to tell you, but I have to ask for a favor first."

"What?"

"You need to say, 'I am a grumpy butthole and I only recently took *some* of the stick out of my ass.'"

"Why would you want or need me to say that?"

"It will be therapeutic. Now say it."

I glared.

"Okay, fine. Just tell me you love me again. But if you say you *think* you love me I'm going to throw *you* off the balcony. So choose your words carefully."

"I love you, Chelsea. Even though I—"

She stepped toward me and pressed her fingers to my mouth. "Nope. Stop while you're ahead. And I love you too, you grumpy asshole." She pulled her hands back and kissed me. "Even though..."

I picked her up, interrupting whatever she'd been about to say with her laughter.

40

EPILOGUE - CHELSEA

~

I ran my hands across my shiny new desk, smiling. There was even a nameplate on my desk that read: Chelsea Cross - Agent.

That's right, bitch. I was an agent now. Certifiably badass. Top of the food chain. The—

My door swung open. Daria stuck her head in, gave me a look like she knew whatever I was thinking was dumb, and cleared her throat. "Wow," she said dryly. "Look at you riding that dick all the way to the top."

If I hadn't gotten to know Daria by now, I might've hurled something at her head for that. Instead, I was smiling. "And what a ride it was."

That earned me a faint smile from Daria. "Your little friend is here. Pathetic, by the way. You made her come just to show off your new office, didn't you?"

"No comment. Send her in, please."

Daria rolled her eyes, then closed my door.

A few moments later, Milly walked into my office. She wasn't wearing athletic gear for a change, which either meant her training session today was much later at night or she'd done it super early this morning. She quickly pulled her hair up in a ponytail and sat down across from my desk, taking in the space. "Very fancy."

"I know. Watch this." I pulled a latch on the front of my desk and stood, lifting the top of my desk up to standing height. It clicked firmly into place. I leaned my elbows on it, smiled, then crashed down when the latch gave out under my weight.

Milly laughed at me. "Wow, Really cool. If you're ever choking in here alone, I'm sure you could use that to propel a hotdog out of your throat."

"Ass," I said, rubbing my chin.

"Then again, you're more of a hotdog in the throat kind of girl, aren't you?"

I balled up a paper from my notepad and tossed it at her. "Is everyone trying to call me some kind of hoe this morning? Did I miss a memo?"

"Sorry, you just make it too fun to tease. But I am proud of you. Seriously, girl. Look at where you are and think about where you came from. You *kicked ass*. And you deserve it."

"Thank you. And for the record, I am a hotdog in the mouth kind of girl."

We both laughed, then Chris stuck his head in my office. "Hey," he said. "Is Damon around?"

"Yeah, why?"

"Shit," Chris said. He pulled his head out of any door and *ran* toward the elevators.

Milly tilted her head at me. "What was that about?"

"With Chris, your guess is as good as mine. He's probably in some fresh trouble."

Before I packed up my things to leave the office, Damon slipped in through my door. He planted his hands on my desk and glared down at me. I made the mistake of telling him a few weeks ago that I'd gotten wet from the sight of that glare alone more than a few times, and now he had weaponized it.

I felt the familiar swirl of heat in my stomach. "Stop that, unless you plan to finish what you're starting."

"I always finish."

I grinned. "Yeah. On my face. On my chest. *On my ass.*"

"Inside you," he added.

I swallowed. I wasn't sure if I was reading too much into it, but I almost wondered if that was some kind of hint. Was he asking if I wanted to try for another baby? *No.* Because that would be insane so soon. Still, the idea of feeling him have his release deep inside me made me want to jump his bones right then and there.

"Is there a reason you're harassing me, Mr. Rose?"

"A few."

"Care to enlighten me?"

He walked around to the back of my chair and put his hands on my shoulders. "This hairstyle isn't appropriate, for starters." Damon fisted my hair and pulled my head back a little roughly so I was looking up at him. He bent low like he was going to kiss me, then moved his lips to my ear. "And your dress is wildly provocative. You're going to distract my staff. You'll have them thinking about tearing off your blouse and sucking your nipples. Of dipping their fingers in you to the knuckles… And I don't permit teasing at Rose Athletic."

"Maybe your employees shouldn't have such dirty minds, Mr. Rose."

He slid a hand down my blouse, even though the blinds on my office windows were open. Thankfully, the few employees who still hadn't left were sitting with the backs to us. "You drive me fucking wild, Chelsea."

I kissed his forearm, grinning to myself. "Good. I like it that way."

"When can I have you to myself?"

"That depends. How long will it take you to close those blinds?"

Among his many talents, Damon Rose was also extremely quick on his feet when properly motivated. I didn't have a stopwatch handy, but I would've clocked his speed to the blinds and back at less than five seconds.

What followed was *not* quick.

41

EPILOGUE - DAMON

~

Ever since I was a kid, there had always been something special about going to the fair. I remembered simpler times, like when Chris was still a middle school athlete catching the eyes of high school coaches and even college recruiters. We'd come to these things and swarms of little middle school fan girls would follow us at a suspiciously close distance.

My parents were always in good moods at the fair. They'd buy us funnel cakes and giant, disgusting legs of turkey on a stick. They'd stuff as many tickets as we could hold into our hands and smile when we wanted to ride the same thing over and over.

It turned out Chelsea had similarly fond memories of fairs, and we'd been meaning to go for months.

We took Luna with us and let her lead the way. We ended up changing strategy after she showed no intentions of ever leaving the game where she got to shoot water at little ducks in kiddie pools. Eventually, we talked her into riding the Ferris wheel.

Chelsea and Luna sandwiched me in the center, and we all

felt the wind blow cool against our hair when the ride started to rotate.

"Are you going to give mommy another baby?" Luna asked.

I held back a smile, then looked to Chelsea who was red-faced with embarrassment.

"That's not really something we should talk about right now, sweetie," Chelsea explained.

"I'd love to give your mom another baby, but it wouldn't be right unless we were married."

"Were you married when you gave me to mommy?" Luna asked.

"Well…" Chelsea was bulging her eyes at me, probably hoping I could save her.

I'd always assumed brutal honesty was the best course with children. "We didn't know you were going to happen when we met, but we're both really happy you did."

Luna giggled. "You're being silly. You have to put me in mommy's belly button to make me. You did too know I was going to happen."

"I was wearing gloves," I said stiffly.

"Was mommy's belly button wearing a glove?"

I looked up at the bright lights of the Ferris wheel, wishing I could think of a way out of this conversation. "Uh…"

"I had a belly plug in. It's like the thing that goes in the sink."

Luna frowned in thought. "So how did I get in, then?"

"Daddy's finger was too big and strong, so it, uh—"

"The point is," I interrupted. I dug in my pocket for the little smooth box. I held it up for Chelsea to see. "If I want to put another baby in your mom's… bellybutton, I've got to put this on her finger, first."

"Oh. Then do it!" Luna said, clapping.

Chelsea's eyes darted between mine and the box. "Is that what I think it is?"

"You know," I said, making like I was about to put it back in my pocket. "Maybe I should think about this a little longer."

Chelsea pinched my shoulder hard enough to sting, then grabbed the box from me. "*Yes.* My answer is yes. And don't you dare even joke about taking this back."

I kissed her, and only stopped because I felt Luna watching. "Does it count if he didn't ask?" she whispered when we pulled apart.

"What?" Chelsea asked.

"He never said, 'will you marry me.' I don't think it counts."

"The ring is what matters," I said. I gestured to the lights and scenery around us. "And the act."

"Hmm," Chelsea worked her lips to the side, staring at the box. "The little one kinda has a point. You need to say the words."

"Marry me," I demanded.

Chelsea waggled her finger and Luna shook her head.

"Manners, daddy."

"I want you to marry me."

"*Ask* her. Don't *tell* her."

I sighed. "Will you marry me?"

Chelsea put her finger to her chin like she needed to think about it.

I groaned and opened the box for her, sliding the ring on her finger. "You will."

"I will," she agreed. "In grumpiness and in health."

-THE END

Want more like this? *My new boss likes rules, but there's one nobody dares to break... No touching his banana. Seriously. The guy is like a potassium addict. Of course, I touched it. If you want to get tech-*

nical, I actually put it in my mouth. Click here to read His Banana now>>

Sign up to my VIP list to get a free copy of one of my books instantly. You'll also get a bonus scene between Damon and Chelsea! Click here>>

Printed in Great Britain
by Amazon